D0321021

School Days

Patrick Chamoiseau was born in Martinique, where he still lives, in 1953. He has published several auto-biographical narratives and various essays which are available in French. He is also the author of three novels: *Chronique des sept misères*, *Solibo magnifique* and *Texaco*, which won France's prestigious Prix Goncourt and has been translated into fourteen languages. Both *Strange Words*, a book of Creole folktales, and *Texaco* are also published by Granta Books.

Also available in English
by Patrick Chamoiseau

Texaco
Strange Words

School Days

Patrick Chamoiseau
Translated
by Linda Coverdale

Granta Books
London

Granta Publications, 2/3 Hanover Yard, London N1 8BE

First published in Great Britain by Granta Books 1998

Copyright © 1994 by Editions Gallimard
Translation © 1997 by the University of Nebraska Press

Publication of this translation was assisted by
a grant from the French Ministry of Culture

All rights reserved. No reproduction, copy or transmissions of this
publication may be made without written permission. No paragraph
of this publication may be reproduced, copied or transmitted save
with written permission or in accordance with the provisions of the
Copyright Act 1956 (as amended). Any person who does any
unauthorized act in relation to this publication may be liable to
criminal prosecution and civil claims for damages.

A CIP catalogue record for this book is
available from the British Library.

1 3 5 7 9 10 8 6 4 2

Printed and bound in Great Britain by
Mackays of Chatham PLC

Learning Resources
Centre

1221138 9

Contents

Preface

One of the liveliest and most creative voices in French literature today is that of Patrick Chamoiseau. Born in 1953 in Fort-de-France, Martinique, where he still lives, he has published several autobiographical narratives (*Antan d'enfance, Chemin-d'école*) in addition to his novels: *Chronique des sept misères, Solibo magnifique,* and *Texaco,* which won France's prestigious Prix Goncourt in 1992. He collaborated with Raphaël Confiant and Jean Bernabé on the critical essay *Éloge de la créolité* and is the coauthor, with Confiant, of *Lettres créoles: Tracées antillaises et continentales de la littérature, 1635–1975.* His other essays include *Martinique* and *Guyane, Traces-mémoires du bagne. Creole Folktales (Au temps de l'antan)* was the first of his works to be translated into English.

Chamoiseau has explored the traditional themes of Caribbean fiction—slavery, colonialism, the development of class and caste distinctions, the collapse of the plantation economy—with an imaginative brio both daring and magisterial. In texts of striking poetic density, he evokes the terrifying destitution at the heart of this lush, tropical world: the loss of ancestral ties to an Africa itself now long gone; the decline of village life and a growing estrangement from the land; the suppression and devaluation of Creole, the everyday language of slavery, in favor of French, the language of the white colonial plantocracy.

In the French Antilles, the language, literature, and culture of France were transmitted to all sectors of society through a strictly metropolitan education, but this increased identification with France came at the cost of further alienation from indigenous folk values. The 1930s, however, saw the birth of the French "black pride" literary movement of *Négritude,* one of whose leaders was the great Martinican poet and politician Aimé Césaire. The postwar decades have been characterized by a search for an original, authentic Caribbean culture, a movement that has led in the French West Indies to a revaluation of *Créolité.* As a writer, Chamoiseau has found resonant themes in the tension between the French and Creole cultures and in the complexities of class, race, and language this tension reveals.

The writer's relationship with the written word—indeed, with the very ability to write—is of paramount interest to Chamoiseau, who embodies the central paradox of Martinican literature: writing necessarily represents a profound break with the essential orality of Creole language and culture. Like Édouard Glissant, the influential literary theoretician of *Antillanité,* Chamoiseau proclaims the need to respect the continuity between the Creole storyteller and the writer as "word maker." He writes in a French that is both highly polished and extravagantly unconventional: antic, lyrical, sarcastic, at times oneiric, even opaque, and above all, *vocal.*

The African griot has been called the repository of the cultural memory of a people. The fabulous narrator of *School Days* recalls to life the cultural memory of a writer-to-be, in the diminutive person of a little black boy of courage and cunning who goes off to school one day with a blithe heart, only to find that he has ventured into a foreign country from which he can never return. When he looks around him, he realizes that in the eyes of his teachers his own world barely exists. Caught betwixt and between, stunned by this *otherness* that has been imposed on him (and on all colonial children everywhere), he nevertheless manages to find his voice, discovering—in both Creole tongue and French text—the awesome healing and subversive powers of language.

ABOUT THE TRANSLATION: Chamoiseau does not believe in glossaries, preferring that his readers open themselves to the "subterranean magic" of strange words, but a short glossary has been appended to this translation to explain a few basic (or irresistibly choice) terms. The author's Creole expressions have been retained, sometimes with English translations provided in footnotes. Perhaps the most important word in *Chemin-d'école* is *négrillon*—a word that is impossible to translate exactly. "Pickaninny" is too pejorative, as is "little nigger boy." "Pickney" is used in the English-speaking Caribbean but for this same reason is closely associated with the literature of that region and would seem jarring in Martinique. "The little black boy," although quite a mouthful, seems closest to the sense of *négrillon* here. Precisely because it is a mouthful, and serene in the knowledge that no reader will forget for a moment that our tiny hero is black, I usually refer to him—with the author's consent—as "the little boy."

Linda Coverdale

School Days

For Guy and Yasmina,
imps of my heart,
musing on the river of honey
that was your moon.

P. C.

Lè ou poèt, fout ou ka pwan fè! . . .
[When you're a poet, is it ever tough! . . .]
Jean-Pierre-Arsaye

May heaven grant that each day
we find something to laugh over
—but without laughing at anyone.
M. J. C., hairdresser

Youngsters,

of the West Indies, of French Guyana, of New Caledonia, of Reunion, of Mauritius, of Rodriguez and other Mascarenes, of Corsica, of Brittany, of Normandy, of Alsace, of the Basque country, of Provence, of Africa, of the four corners of the Orient, of all national terrortories, of all far-flung dominions, of all outlying posts of empires or federations, you who have had to face a colonial school, yes, you who in other ways are still confronting one today, and you who will face this challenge tomorrow in some other guise: This voice of bitter laughter at the One and Only—a firmly centered voice challenging all centers, a voice beyond all home countries and peacefully diversal in opposition to the universal—is raised in your name.

In Creole friendship,
P. C.

Longing

My brothers and sisters O! I have something to tell you: the little black boy made the mistake of begging for school. I must add, in his defense, that his suckling days were long gone and that by exploring the endless possibilities of his home, he had wrung them dry. This humble conquistador now developed a taste for window sills. There he spied on the hustle and bustle of the street, jealously watching other black children strolling by without mamas or papas. He was the first to volunteer whenever someone had to dash off to the store to fetch a bit of salt meat or fish needed by his mama, Mam Ninotte. Sticking out his chest but blinking nervously just the same, he would scoot across the street like a sneaky mongoose, glance boldly into the Syrian merchants' booths, and for no good reason, once out of sight of Mam Ninotte leaning from her window, he would suddenly stand still—blip!—to gaze wide-eyed at life. To any onlooker, he must have seemed a fledgling tumbled from a low-hanging bough. His staring eyes were so brimful of anxious innocence that folks thought him struck with congenital idiocy. Good souls would come up to him and say, *Well, my lil' one, why are you standing here in such surprise? Say, where's your mama, h'm?* And in a twinkling he would change into a cloud of dust uncatchable at any speed. He'd zigzag through the passing throng, bounce over the merchants' baskets, slam headfirst into big butts sashaying along the street, trample the one sound toe of some achy old nigger, and clatter into the shop more winded than a broken-down accordion.

And terrified to boot.

I now summon the *Répondeurs* . . .

He skulked back from the shop with his purchase, hugging the walls, looking at no one, all the more panicky because he knew no other way home. Sure enough: his groaning victims were waiting for him. Over here, a rudely jostled shopkeeper still craned her neck to find that little bugger who'd stirred up her rheumatics, and over there, an oldster in his Sunday best brandished a new shoe on high, displaying his swollen toe with vengeance in his eye. The boy had no choice but to steal through the crowd, as oh-so-tiny as an ant, slinking slier than a slippery-slidy skink, turning almost to salt as he reached the danger zone where tempers flared into proclamations of terrible revenge. By happy chance, none of the avengers could see any connection between the apocalyptic dust cloud and the trembly little ashen-faced black boy.

Such adventures gave the child food for thought for eleventy-seven eternities. Certain that his victims were yet on the look-out for him, he would decide to lie low. No one at home could fathom his reluctance to set foot back out into the street or even anywhere near the window sills. He would become a model of the very finest decorum. Most quiet. Best behaved. And obedient. Not one spark of insolence in that limpid eye. Mam Ninotte, an expert in this field, would heave a great sigh. *Sweet Jesus, what deviltry has this scamp been up to now?* Distrustfully, she would count the matches, check the demijohn of kerosene, inspect her pots of marmalade, and peek under the beds in search of some silent disaster, never suspecting that the Beast had begun to strike in the great wide world outside.

Outside . . . the street . . . and even farther away . . . sweet song of the horizon — it was all this that he now craved. He was no longer content with trips to the movies and Sunday strolls on which the Big Kids dragged him along by one wing. He wanted to go *by himself*. But go where? In what direction? He had nowhere to go, and no one had commissioned him to wander. His brief forays to the shop and back had finally lost their savor of excitement. It no longer made him jump when someone along the way would ask, *And jus' where are you off to, my son?* He now knew how to restrain his fears to a twitchy eyelid or an icy-cold sweat. Nothing startled him anymore into those breathless dashes that had given rise in the Rue François-Arago to the legend of a shin-barking zombie. He had tried his hand at modest explorations, venturing beyond the shop, braving on his own the mayhem of the fish market when the boats came in. He had even, one expeditionary day, observed the customary riot at la Croix-Mission, where the share-taxis disgorged their rustic hordes. He could have strayed even farther afield. But it was impossible: Mam Ninotte had laid down a law that weighed on his conscience. He felt born to wander, but Mam Ninotte cursed such proclivities every blessed day. *Spare me,* she told her boys, *spare me two things: that I should ever have to visit you in jail, or learn you've taken to straggling footloose like stray cur-dogs . . . No vagabonds in my house, you hear me, you gentlemen there!?**

So the little boy sat stewing in the lost enchantment of home. Even worse, the Big Kids started going off somewhere each morning. At first, only his eldest sister, nicknamed the Baroness, set out like that. As time passed, his second sister, Marielle, began to follow her. Then came the turn of Jojo the Math Whiz, eldest of his big brothers, and finally Paul the Musician joined them all. Mam Ninotte dressed them sprucely, and while the youngest watched, his brothers and sisters — strictly

---

* *Répondeurs*: We hear you! We hear you!

disciplined by the implacable Baroness — would vanish over the horizon carrying strange bags (. . . *beyond the grocery store yes, beyond the marketplace yes, beyond la Croix-Mission yes* . . .). They would reappear at noon, to eat, and leave again, returning only at dusk. The little boy stayed home alone with Mam Ninotte, who would sit down to her sewing in the tranquil apartment. He'd roam here and there, hunting for some last trace of enchantment clinging to the stairwell or the roof over the cooking area out in the courtyard; he'd strive to find the old amazement in a spider, rat, or dragonfly . . . But, *awa*! Everything seemed picked clean. He paced across bitter silences, insipid stillnesses, deserts that none of his mischief would ever bring to life again. And whenever he sought refuge in himself, the seat of his omnipotence, he came up against the same obsession: *to go.*

But where?

One day, he explained to Mam Ninotte that he wanted to go with the Big Kids.

" 'Scuse me?"

"To go."

"Where to?" inquired Mam Ninotte uneasily.

"To go."

"To go in which direction, h'm? I'm too old for riddles," said Mam Ninotte impatiently. (Actually, she dreaded becoming entangled in one of those strings of questions he could reel off with maddening expertise.)

"I want to go with the Big Kids to where they go . . ."

"Do you know where they go, h'm?"

"I want to go."

"Don't worry, no fear, you'll go . . ."

"Go where?" he asked quickly, hoping to find out at last.

Then, with the utmost gravity, and with a strict look in her eye (plus something like a gleam of hope), Mam Ninotte whispered in his ear, "To school."

Répondeurs:
In the kitchen courtyard
Three silences stand guard
You conk them all about
But silence wins out
Oh so clever
Bored as ever.

And yet, the Big Kids never moped after school. They seemed happy to return to the nest. As soon as they got home, they relaxed, made themselves comfortable, as though they'd just reached port in a storm. They greedily invaded the two rooms, frisking joyfully around Mam Ninotte, clinging to her and bombarding her with words while she fixed them a four o'clock of stale bread, margarine, and hard sausage. Their pleasure at being home was so all-encompassing that they even seemed thrilled to see their calamitous little brother again: they kissed him, caressed his nubby hair, humored his silliness for a good second or even two. This unusual attitude should have tipped him off, but *awa*! the tiny recluse saw nothing in their beaming faces but a future stuffed with promise.

The other mystery was those bags they lugged around everywhere. The one belonging to the Baroness was fat and heavy; Marielle's was a little less so; from Jojo to Paul these enigmatic objects grew even thinner. Each child protected his or her bag ferociously. Their little brother was sent flying more than once for attempting to get his hands on these prizes.

One day, he decided to out-shout them all.

Grabbing Paul's bag, he darted under a bed, shrieking, *It's mine! It's mine!* as though trying to convince himself first of all. Impervious to the magical virtue of these cries, Paul prepared to settle that dirty stinker's hash but good. Mam Ninotte wasn't around, so it was the Baroness who saved his life by checking Paul's homicidal fury. Then she introduced under the bed a long, slender, and formidable hand that brought the culprit to his senses then and there. He emerged blubbering from his hiding place and gave up the bag to Paul. But listen closely!* That mulish child made himself into the martyr of the century. He wept single-mindedly for thirty-three days and thirty-three nights straight without even pausing for breath. Only a bowl of fresh milk or a shaving of chocolate brought any relief from this insufferable racket. As a finishing touch to his despair, he came up with a pasty complexion, tummy aches, and what looked like smallpox. Some said it was mumps; others, prickly heat or an unknown plague. He went shaky at the knees and fluttery at the eyelids, and just to cap things off, his familiar asthma became suddenly ungovernable and sent him into death throes every night. Mam Ninotte, her nerves at the snapping point, finally bought him his very own bag (or more precisely, as he would learn later on, a school satchel). A small rectangle of red plastic sporting a handle and a dainty metal catch. O satchel of great mystery! Inside he discovered a short stick of white chalk, a cardboard-framed slate, and a sponge in the cutest round box.

Sheer delight.

Répondeurs:
Beautiful dream!

They watched him strut about the apartment, showing off his satchel. They watched him take on the majestic bearing of a

* *Répondeurs*: Oh, closely!

senator, a pope, a star-of-stage-and-screen with furrowed brow. They watched him talk to himself, gesturing grandly. They watched him in his more vulnerable moments, opening his satchel and contemplating with a glazed eye the incomprehensible slate, the incomprehensible chalk, the incomprehensible sponge, then shutting everything up again as though he were padlocking a treasure chest. They watched him sob and beg to be dressed in the morning, watched him snatch up his satchel and follow the Big Kids to the door, where Mam Ninotte would tenderly restrain him. Then he would whimper at a window sill, watching them disappear without him, draining the bitter cup of abandonment to the very last drop.

Répondeurs:
Lookit the senator
Wop wop wipe that sponge around!

By opening his satchel and fiddling with its contents, he made some discoveries. The chalk showed up nicely on the blackness of the slate.

He drew a line.
Then two.
Then a thousand circles.
Then a bunch of scribbles.

When both sides were covered, he learned how to erase them. With his hand. His elbow. His shoulders. Until he was white everywhere and in tears over his used-up chalk. When it came to chalk, however, the Big Kids weren't stingy. They had loads of it, in all colors. And so the little boy returned to his doodling with a piece of white chalk and a green one, too. Then the Baroness offered him a stub of red chalk. He obtained a yellow stick from Marielle in return for a few moments' peace. And Jojo, appalled to find him erasing his slate with his hair, taught him the secret of the sponge. From then on, he was to be found stretching on his tiptoes and dangling from the sink, hovering around the water bottles, busy with the courtyard faucet, anxiously soaking his tiny sponge, which was never wet enough to suit him. Not for even one moment did he ever have enough chalk, enough sponge, enough slate. You can take my word for it!

The age of petroglyphs dawned. Having accidentally discovered how beautifully the apartment walls lent themselves to the magic of chalk, he soon covered them with it. Mam Ninotte, accustomed though she was to devastations, flew right off the handle. She chased him around and around, wondering aloud what she could possibly have done to the Goodlord to deserve this. She nabbed her son by the scruff, intending to administer a sound thrashing, but found herself no match for his wiles. This little monster excelled in making himself suddenly frail, flimsy, fragile. Seized by the collar, he became a quaking chicky. He knew how to flood his eyes with discomfiting distress. The invincible Mam Ninotte was vanquished on the spot. She spent the next hour washing down the walls and describing to him in detail what tortures he would suffer if ever he did that again. *Ou pa ni an ti tablo* — *You've got your slate, haven't you?!* But the slate had lost all its charm. Now the walls alone cast a spell upon him. So he took refuge in the somewhat gloomy hall shared by all the apartments. There no one worried about the state of the walls. And there he was to be found from then on: inspired, hieratic, important, unflagging, covering the hardwood paneling with a proliferation of messy scrawls that he — and he alone — found simply dazzling.

The other advantage of chalk was that it tasted good. The prehominid would often cut short an artistic impulse in favor of a little nibble. The paneling had to make do with some unfinished works. There were also silent dramas: should he save that last bit of chalk for his next masterpiece or eat it right up? *So hard to choose!* But such quandaries were brief: that childish imagination was ignorant of tomorrow and all time to come.

Répondeurs:
The walls have preserved
the age of petroglyphs.
Oh, I can still see them!
I can still see myself . . .

O humble relics, be my *Répondeurs* . . .

Répondeurs:
Inscribe, scribe!
Scriven without scribbling!
Inscribe!

Go ahead, laugh to see me haunting all these shipwrecks, a salvager leaving sumptuous silver plate behind, not too handy with the net, rather clumsy with fishhooks, bending over you with such care and concern . . .

. . . and now see, memory, how I confront you no longer, I inhale your shimmering spindrift hanging motionless in soaring flight . . . O silent tumult of a life going by . . . Did you laugh to see me attempt an embrace, like some mooncalf drooping over his own shadow?

. . . the idea is to remain anchored in oneself, in that esteem first praised by the poet,* attentive not to one's self but to its incessant movement . . . always imperceptible . . .

*Saint John Perse, *Éloges.* (Translator's note.)

In that esteem . . .

. . . faint hails . . . O sedimentary sensations . . . awakenings to the world that are mere feelings now . . . heaps of tears and fears . . . sculptors of body and soul . . . you who have crafted a human memory in the living flesh . . . see, he summons you, still at a loss, as bereft as ever, hardly more stalwart before you than in those tender years of wonder . . . Here is my command: Answer me! . . .

The age of petroglyphs in no way diminished the little black boy's longing for school. On the contrary. The Big Kids sometimes snatched away his chalk and painstakingly inscribed somefin' on a wall out in the hall. And this somefin' seemed decipherable. It could be *said*. His own scribblings inspired sounds, feelings, sensations that he expressed however he pleased but always differently: their interpretation depended on his mood and the ambiance of the moment. The marks the Big Kids made, however, seemed to contain some intangible meaning, which any Big Kid could decode at any time, whereas they scrunched up their faces in bewilderment at their little brother's scrawls. This mystery of meaning deepened quickly and very nearly took a tragic turn. Here's how . . .

Jojo the Math Whiz had picked up this same penchant for decorating the hallway. Chalk in hand, he'd join the scribbler out in the corridor, and in the space above the pipsqueak's reach, he'd line up the cabalistic numbers he seemed to love as much as life itself. The proximity of this big brother reinforced the youngster's doodling frenzy, but having such a pest buzzing about his ankles must have put a sizable crimp in the Math Whiz's numerical ecstasy. Always clever at cruelty, Jojo found a way to clip those wings. He carefully wrote out something-or-other right under his little brother's nose.

"Guess whazzat . . ."

"Whazzat?"

"That there is your first name . . . an' you're inside it!" he revealed, with a wizard's mocking grin.

Wo yoyoy! . . . Jojo the Math Whiz had just plunged the little boy into a fine predicament: he saw himself there, captured whole within a chalk mark. *Which meant he could be erased from the world!* Pretending he wasn't scared shitless (which would have tickled Jojo), he began to copy out his first name a thousand times, in order to proliferate and avoid a genocide. Copying was hard. And slow. Frowning with concentration, he had to keep his mind in the same spot. His hand found itself stumbling over those closed shapes that twisted in on themselves, devoid of dash or energy. The movements lacked all majesty. But, since they concerned him so closely, these forms — bit by little bit — began to swell with meaning, to seem more powerful than the lightning strokes he'd tossed off hitherto . . .

Discovery: he held the chalk with his entire hand (either one), like a dagger. Then, one hand turned out to be more skillful than the other. Then, it became clear that holding the chalk with the tips of certain fingers was easiest of all. *Mama-Mama-Mama!*

So he took to trapping scraps of reality inside his chalk marks. He began begging to have people write out first names, then words he supplied, then noises he made. He wanted signs for dogs, cats, cars, noses, eyes, ears. You'd think he might have stopped there. But, always given to extremes, he demanded of whoever passed through the hallway that they mark down the whole universe in one go. The first person waylaid was Paul, who wasn't one to rack his brains. The second was Mam Ninotte, who asked him testily to get out from underfoot. The third, resplendent in his mailman's uniform, was the Papa, who quickened his pace and seemed not to hear. Only the Math Whiz vouchsafed him an enigmatic reply. He drew two tiny Siamese-twin circles and snarled imperiously, *Everything's there: that's infinity . . .*

This ability to capture pieces of the world seemed to come from school. No one had confirmed this, but the chalk, the satchel, the morning departure toward this unknown place seemed linked to a ritual of power into which he longed to be initiated. And so, each and every day, he clamored to go to school.* *Clamored* is a weak word. Let's say he plagued Mam Ninotte's existence, dogged her every footstep like her own personal misfortune, tripped up her broom, interrupted her laundry songs, transformed her ironing into a nightmare in slow motion. When she settled herself with pleasure at her sewing machine (that delightful refuge for a quiet sit-down), the Impious One harassed her still. She couldn't even fly into a temper; her fat arms would shudder to a halt in mid-flight over the sudden frailty of her littlest, and the mighty breath of a bellow, choked off—flap!—would sigh away into a lengthy supplication to the heavens above. *O Saint Michael, give me peace!*

"Mama . . ."

"Huh! Good God Almighty!"

"Mama . . ."

"Sweet Jesus, forgive us our trespasses . . ."

"Mama . . ."

"Blind, deaf, and dumb from birth, that's me. That's just how I am . . ."

"Mama . . ."

"Forget about me . . ."

**Répondeurs: He clamored fit to bust!*

"Mama . . ."

"Blessed are the persecuted, for theirs is the kingdom of heaven!"

"Mama . . ."

"Who's calling me, huh?"

"It's me . . ."

"You're not going to reduce me to a rackabones with this school business, are you? Do you understand me, huh!?"

"I din' say anyt'ing . . ."

"So much the better . . ."

"Mama . . ."

Répondeurs:
Rackabones!

When Mam Ninotte informed him he would be going off to school bright-and-early the next morning, he was speechless. Such good news did not relieve this poor mama's martyrdom for long: the Tormentor wanted to know why tomorrow and not right now? What time would he leave? Wearing what clothes? Would he have to put on shoes? And his school satchel wasn't really big enough after all and he preferred Paul's, et cetera, et cetera . . . Mam Ninotte replied patiently, then simply clammed up. But once off and running, he could rattle away for hours unfazed by anyone's stubborn silence.

The day before the first day of school dragged on forever. Sun took its time to rise, then set out on a lackadaisical stroll. The morning gave birth to long, pregnant hours that whiled themselves away by knitting to the drowsy rhythm of a rocking chair. Noon was a steady stare. As for the afternoon, that moment of deep tranquility, it starched the world with thick blasts of heat. Frantic with anticipation, the Impatient One tried to speed up time. In those days, to hurry life along you simply took a nap. Sleep and dreams would swallow up the languor of daytime. You'd awaken at the far end of a great seven-league leap. His head all in a whirl, the little boy went to bed to flit across the afternoon and streak through the night . . .

Répondeurs:
Time
brings us different times
and leaves other times behind . . .

Next morning he was wide awake in no time. Mam Ninotte didn't even have to threaten him with a pot of cold water. He sprang to attention, all sweetness and light. He got dressed along with everyone else. At the front door, Mam Ninotte did not hold him back. She took his hand and off they went in one direction while the Big Kids set out in another. The two of them headed for the Canal Levassor, which they crossed on the curve of the Pont Gueydon to reach the right bank. Unexplored territories, glimpsed from afar. He held tight to his mama's hand and swung his satchel as though it were a censer in a procession. His head was spinning with fear and excitement. They came to a trim little house, where they joined other mamas and youngsters in a hall leading to a large room. There, instantly unforgettable, stood his first teacher: Mam Salinière.

Répondeurs:
Mam Salinière
the clamorous yawls
churn up the canal
Oh, the fishing boats are in!
You
a queen on your threshold

one eye on the children
a wave of your hand
brings you the promise of redfish
Oh, the fishing boats are in!

She was a plump mulatta, gray-haired, perhaps, with pleasing features and a gentle disposition. She presided over a dining room containing rows of wooden desks into which were set leaden inkwells, whose purpose the little boy would learn only long afterward, for here they were always empty. The desks and benches were sturdy, black with age, stained and scratched all over. They seemed pensive. Everything was going well. Mam Salinière spoke kindly to him. She touched his hair, exclaimed at the beauty of his satchel. She bestowed the same welcome on each of her young charges, but the little boy felt he was her favorite.

Then tragedy struck.

Suddenly Mam Salinière's hand took the place of Mam Ninotte's. Led into the room, the little boy found himself installed on one of the benches. *Ayayayayaye!* Mam Ninotte had left him! . . . She had vanished down the hall! . . . Gone down to the river! . . . Crossed back over the bridge! . . . Gone! . . . Gone! . . . Gone! . . . Most certainly forever! . . . He who had so often pretended to be in despair was crushed to find himself really there. But he didn't cry, or run away, or scream. He decided to change into a stone and wait, petrified, for his mama to return. Mam Salinière, who in the course of her long career had had to cope with all sorts of shenanigans, discovered that day that it was possible for certain children to spend a whole morning without talking, breathing, blinking, hearing, seeing, or even trembling, as impenetrable as a shard of volcanic rock. And with eyes just as unfathomable.

Answer me . . .

Mam Ninotte's reappearance at eleven o'clock restored him to life. On the way back, he remained tight-lipped, as though stunned silent by betrayal. Mam Ninotte, the traitress, asked a thousand questions without getting boo from him. Going home — to his chalk, his walls, his hideaway — was just as sweet as could be. On first days of school, Mam Ninotte would always cook up something tasty, running a tab for steak and fries or grilled lamb chops with yellow bananas. Almost unheard-of dishes that made up for first-day nerves. At the table, the Big Kids made a fuss over the new schoolboy and congratulated him on his recent promotion. They questioned him, but now that he had the floor for once, the little monster had nothing to say.

After lunch, having digested his apprehension, he was a tad less eager to go back to that place. Seeing the Big Kids set out again put some heart into him. He tried to get Mam Ninotte to say she'd stay with him on one of Mam Salinière's benches. Mam Ninotte, without promising a thing, took him firmly in hand. Once again he wound up abandoned to the liturgies of the nice lady. Even though he fixed the most pitiable of dying eyes on Mam Ninotte, she went off anyway. This time, he didn't change himself completely into stone but left an eye and an ear free. He heard songs. He saw games. He caught himself clapping his hands. He found himself carried away by an unfamiliar pleasure: the company of other little black children like himself (actually, they were multicolored: *chabins*, *koulis*, *cacos*, mulattos, *chi-chines*, *békés-goyave* ... but he didn't notice), of the same size, height, and language, quick to understand him. The world spread out before him prospects of complicity.

Mam Salinière gave him some paper and colored pencils. She showed him strange images of snow and sang lilting ditties from Brittany or Provence. Sometimes she stopped everything for a snack of milk and cookies.

Then they'd start singing again.

And then they'd play.

And then they'd draw.

One day, Mam Salinière tacked some big letters on her small blackboard. In the attentive hush, she chanted, *A B C D . . .* The children chorused back to her, *A B C D*. All the fervor of childhood was in these warbled notes. In those days, you sang with your soul. You became one with the song, and the song was heartfelt. The little boy had heard his mother sing. He'd even tried out a few of her verses himself, and he remembered the Creole counting rhymes she'd murmured to him when he was sick in bed. But there, with Mam Salinière, in that universe centered around him, his enthusiasm was boundless, fearless, unquestioning. When she opened her arms, gracefully marking time with her hands, he felt enchanted, and he sang, he sang Aaaaa Béééé Céééé Déééééé . . .

Another day, Mam Salinière asked them to make those letters on their slates and display them when she clapped her hands. At first the little boy thought to win admiration by presenting one of his scribble-scrabbles instead. But Mam Salinière showed no reaction. She ignored him and congratulated others. On the next try, though, when he offered her his version of an *A* (more or less: two lines coming together up top, going apart at the bottom, and tied together — tiak!), she suddenly discovered him, went into raptures, told him *Braaaaavo!* This episode transformed him into an expert scribe of the capital *A* and the lowercase *a*. This new *homo sapiens* took his work home with him. With chalk, nails, and coal, he inscribed *A* and *a* on each step of the staircase, on the handrail, and on every baluster; he put some on the thresholds of all the doors and did not spare the walls out in the hallway. Only a stern look from Mam Ninotte (despite her pleasure at seeing him writing on his own) prevented him from demonstrating what he had learned upon the cupboard, the four chairs, the table — and its cloth. As for the Big Kids, they remained indifferent to this burst of erudition. The *homo sapiens* was not in the least disappointed by their obscurantism. From suppertime to bedtime he inflicted upon them the song of enlightenment: *a a a a a a a a A, a a AAA aa aaa AAA aaa* . . . The Benighted Ones had to beg Heaven to send him to sleep.

Répondeurs:
Knuckle soup!
Greens soup!
Lean Friday soup!
Who doesn't want to grow up?

School was fun. He was always in a hurry to get there. Mam Salinière made everything entertaining. She was another sort of Mam Ninotte, equally kind and generous with her affection. Her strictness was not threatening but briskly protective. Her anger was merely a raised eyebrow. And her only punishment was indifference. Now the little boy had two mamas, or rather, he slipped from Mam Ninotte to Mam Salinière without a pang. In fact, the schoolmistress seemed to be learning from her young pupils. He felt as though he were teaching her things; he could amaze her by drawing a letter, by caterwauling Do-Re-Mi-Fa-Sol, by drawing a witch, an apple tree, a pine, a snowflake, by mixing two colors together to make a new one. She was thrilled to see him cutting things out with scissors, pasting pictures, painting, erasing. Everything he did was lovely, clever, brave. The problem was that whatever the other children did (dreadful retards he usually considered utter stumblebums) was just as lovely, clever, and brave. Whenever he had the feeling he was being silly, Mam Salinière never saw him, never heard him. In her world, foolishness got you nowhere. So he saved most of his nonsense for home, where it flourished nicely.

Still, once they had an awful fright. A rowdy brat did a really bad thing one day. Like what? Probably sticking a pencil in someone's eye or bloodying a nose with a wild swing. Mam Salinière lost her temper, raised her voice, and dragged the offender over to a dark, tiny closet, theretofore invisible, hidden beneath the stairs. She made sure the children got a good look at it.

The dungeon!

Whoever was clapped into the dungeon, she explained, stayed kneeling there in darkness as long as a Sleeping Beauty. You couldn't whine, or whimper, or let out one blessed peep. Staring at this dungeon bad-as-hell, the culprit began to snivel. The black hole looked like the gaping jaws of those dragons whose existence the youngsters had recently discovered. They thought they heard the howling of those wolves that would course forever after through their imaginations. They returned to their places, silent and wobbly-legged. Nobody ever did anything really bad again. And that's the truth.

Mam Salinière, I have only the wispiest memories of you. Your name. Your genteel manners. Your benevolent patience. My hands clapping while you sing. Yours keeping the beat while I sing. Our snack of bread and jam. Our naps in the sultry afternoon heat, while you watched our eyelids. I've forgotten the sound of your voice, the cut of your dresses, the shape of your hands, your smell . . . but these things nourish the quiet splendor of a tenderness I can't put into words. Well, that's settled: never mind the others—I was her favorite after all!

Soon, the little boy was able to go to Mam Salinière's house by himself and return home the same way. At first Mam Ninotte walked him to the bridge. Then she began turning back before reaching it. Then she just watched him cross from her window. Then she simply kissed him goodbye when he left with the Big Kids. From the house to the store; from the house to Mam Salinière's: he had two routes at his command. He was beginning to *go* . . . It didn't take him long to add a third to his repertoire: from Mam Salinière's to the store. The world was getting bigger, amazin' . . .

At Mam Salinière's house, he learned things to fuel interminable monologues with Mam Ninotte. He could babble about the wicked fairy Carabosse, the Seven Dwarfs, mermaids, apples, pears, a certain Frère Jacques who was snoozing, his friend Pierrot-prête-moi-ta-plume. He was familiar with the problems of Princess Aurora. He reeled off the seasons: summer, fall, winter, spring. He could draw the Eiffel Tower, trains, bales of hay. He explained to Mam Ninotte that witches flew around on long brooms, and on these broomsticks they could whoosh down the chimney into your house . . . He reassured her by revealing the existence of good fairies who dispensed happiness with a touch of their magic wands. Mam Ninotte was enraptured by his immense learning, even if she did frown on discovering he was drawing their home surrounded by oaks and fir trees and crowned with a smoking chimney. *'Scuse me?!*

The Papa observed this boy wonder from afar. School did not seem all that important to him. The little boy had often heard him tell the Baroness that at such places, you went in a sheep only to come out a goat. He found his youngest son's learning irrelevant. He listened with a jaunty air to the child's nattering and interrupted his display of wisdom with a song: *The busy-*

bee bookworms beetle off to school, but . . . Baa-baa! And this bleating amused him no end . . . but his son didn't feel like a goat, he felt like a schoolboy. The pride gleaming in Mam Ninotte's eyes proved it to him.

The Papa, squinting uneasily at one of the chimney-topped houses his youngest was doodling all over the place, consulted Mam Ninotte: *Am I imagining things, Gros Kato, or is this brat of yours turning our shack into a gigantic boiler?*

It was Paul who revealed the awful truth to him. The little boy had picked a fight with his older brother, first comparing their school satchels, then probably declaring his school superior to all others and his teacher the absolute best. Whereupon Paul, instead of being crestfallen, replied treacherously, "Well, you don't even go to real school, anyway!"

"Huh?! So what is it?"

"A poky lil' nursery school! Where you play tea party and sing stupid stuff . . ."

The little boy was crushed.

The investigation was painful. Mam Ninotte, of course, swore up and down that he went to school at Mam Salinière's house. *So if it's not school it's what? A fish market?* When he asked Marielle (she was combing her long *kouli* hair), the reply was less than clear: *It's a kind of school . . .* Noticing his distress, the Baroness tried to be pragmatic: *The important thing is that you learn how to be less of a jerk . . .* Between two columns of figures, Jojo the Math Whiz stabbed him to the heart. School was a lot tougher than the monkey business at Mam Salinière's . . . Too absorbed in a seven-layer formula to provide further details, however, Jojo quickly sent him packing. Now he had to approach Paul again. Since they were at war, he had to make a peace offering, in the form of a sweet. When the enemy was deep in ecstasy over his candy, the little boy asked him just what school was, exactly. *You dope,* his brother told him pompously, *school is where you learn lessons, so if you come home to Mama without twenty-two pages of homework to do—then it jus' ain't school* ...

"Mama ..."

"H'm?"

"I want to go to school ..."

"Good God Almighty—he's starting up again!" howled Mam Ninotte, appalled.

And she swarmed through the apartment in search of the facety troublemaker who had lied to the child like that. So varied and persuasive were her threats that his brothers and sisters filed past him groaning, *It's school, don't worry, s'all right, you're in school, it's school, it's school* ... Small consolation.

The next time he saw Mam Salinière, he asked her for some homework to do. Unaware of what was at stake, she replied, *You'll have plenty of time for all that, my boy, when you go off to school* ...

His new life came apart at the seams.

Once again he found himself unfledged, a chick in the nest. He hid his sorrow behind the pleasure of carrying his satchel, of still passing for a schoolboy in the eyes of the Syrian merchants who saw him go by, of setting out at the same time as the Big Kids, of coming home around noon with his head bowed to show any skeptics that it was heavier on the return trip. As a finishing touch to the subterfuge, he wangled an exercise book from Mam Ninotte and was discovered nodding drowsily over it, wiped out by the imaginary lessons he was struggling to learn. When Paul found him like that, sitting with his head in his hands, he yelped, *Lordy, this nitwit doesn't have to do homework and he wants some anyway!* Which, in the opinion of all the Big Kids, went way beyond stupidity and kept on going . . .

The Papa to Mam Ninotte: *Whoa, this kid is drawing apples in the middle of mango season! He needs a soothing mint bath!*

Répondeurs:
Lovely zigs!
Ugly zags!
Around the next corner,
the best is yet to come!

Memory, I see: Mam Salinière is fading. There is no departure, no farewell. She does not say, *My children, you will be leaving.* She does not say, *Remember me in the big school.*

Nothing.

Some times pass.

The little black boy finds himself hand in hand again with Mam Ninotte and carrying another satchel.

Gray day.

Misty drizzle.

Shivery wind.

He walks beside his brother Paul: they're going in a different direction. They arrive in front of a great wooden barracks of a place sporting a flag: blue-white-red. There, throngs of little boys and mamas mill around in a turmoil of prattling, shouting, blubbering. Each child is stiff-as-a-stick in starchy splendor, feeling the pinch of new shoes. Each child's hair has been clipped right down to the scalp. Each child is fragrant with *Ploum-Ploum* and *Étoile*. The building is huge, towering several stories high, reaching for the sky.

A bell rings; the crowd surges forward. Mam Ninotte leads him into a small courtyard where a man standing on a table calls the roll. When his turn comes, Paul goes to join other children in a double line. The little boy clutches Mam Ninotte's hand even more tightly. He hears his name. The world falls to pieces. Mam Ninotte pushes him toward another man, who has him line up along with other anxious youngsters. And he hears the first instruction from his new Teacher: *Hold hands with your partner, gentlemen . . .*

Répondeurs:
Gray day.
Mizzle-drizzle . . .
Back to school
That's a dampener
Downtown smells of wet wood
rain-buckled cardboard . . .

Once again Mam Ninotte is leaving, abandoning him to this suddenly hostile universe. He's not the center of anything, just one among many. He must look sharp, because no kindness is poised to envelop him. The Teacher has none of Mam Salinière's gentleness; he seems more like a cowherd. He scrutinizes the row of children, slicing the air with both hands and closing one eye to direct them into a straight line. He studies each face with wary interest, as though he had to cross a nest of red ants and were trying to gauge their warlike temper.

The classroom was on the ground floor of the École Perrinon. The room was flanked on one side by the boys' playground and on the other, glimpsed through half-open blinds, by the playground of the adjacent girls' school. The room was huge. The blackboard, enormous. The atmosphere was frightening, severe, echoing, anonymous. Far from the calm of Mam Salinière's house. Nothing and nobody would coddle them here. With sinking heart the little boy—no fool—shunned the front benches and hid out at the far end of the classroom. Sitting with his back to the wall afforded him protection on that side plus a broad view of this disquieting situation. Brows knitted, cheeks sucked in, an acrid tongue: he felt trapped in the very bottom of a net.

The rest of the flock weren't any better off. He could sense their clammy anxiety. They stared at one another and stole glances at the Teacher, trying to avoid his eye. He was bustling around his desk with an attendance book. He would leave to check on something, return, sign some papers, leave again without paying any attention to his rigidly apprehensive captives. The entire building reverberated with the sound of Big Kids tramping upstairs to their classrooms. You heard chairs scraping, windows creaking, commands, shouts, objects falling over. Everything seemed to be awakening from a kind of lethargy. You could still see a few mamas in the courtyard conversing with *Monsieur le Directeur*, whom each new boy would soon learn to dread. Then the tumult died away. The caretaker swung the entrance gate shut with a lugubrious clang.

The silence began to weigh heavily. Finishing his paperwork, the Teacher stepped to the head of the class and addressed them solemnly: *Our prresent difficulties notwithstanding, allow me, gentlemen, to extend a grracious welcome to you without furrther ado . . .*

Everyone felt positively sick.

When the Teacher began calling the roll, the little boy started to suffocate. When you heard your name, you had to stand up, nod, and sing out clearly, *Present!* These requirements were just too much for most of the children, and most particularly for the little boy, who was devoting all his energy to clenching his whole body into one bundle of nerves and helplessly amplifying his anguish at being abandoned by Mam Ninotte. *O traitress!* Besides, his knees were knocking. His legs had turned into slender grass blades incapable of supporting him. The Teacher went down the list, ticking off first and last names. Those called stood up, one after another. And the little boy began to notice things. A few of the children still had breath enough to speak. Their responses reflected a hint of spirit and even pride at being there. Others, more numerous, bleated out a pathetic gurgling. Some rose silently and plopped back down like a mango clipped from its bough by a well-aimed stone. Two-or-three, instead of the required *Present*, produced a garbled *Pwezent* . . . The Teacher, merciless, would zero in on them: *I beg your pardon?*

" . . . Pre . . . sent . . ."

"Ye gods of Olympus, that sounds like an old man's death rrattle! Put some heart into it, boys!"

"Present!"

"That's better!"

" . . . sent . . ."

"We're swallowing syllables?! We didn't have enough to eat this morning? Rrepeat that if you please . . ."

"Pr . . . sent . . ."

"The *e*, my friend, is tonic, it's strressed! *Prreh*-sent, for heaven's sake!"

"Preh-sent!"

"Ah, *that's* more like it . . ."

" . . . Prst . . ."

"That is all the effect your name prroduces? You should be prroud to have a name, you thoughtless boy, you should shout it out loud, because not too long ago, let me tell you, we were slaves and had no names at all! Prronounce it clearly!"

"Present!"

"Well done!"

At the sound of his name, the little boy sprang up like a rubber band, stammered out his *Pwezent,* and snapped back into his seat, crouching down behind the child in front of him. There, panting, he awaited the end of the world. The Teacher, alas, had not spotted him in time and now looked around inquisitively. *Do my ears deceive me? Might our classroom be haunted by a phantom prresence after the manner of Rroncevaux, which ever since the death of valiant Rroland, strikes fear into the passing trraveler? Show yourself, please* . . . Half dead, the little boy rose, pressed his stomach against the desk to steady himself, and stood slump-shouldered, with lolling head and raggedy breath.

"What is your name?"

At the sound of his name, tiny chuckles sputtered from some of the other children in spite of their collective terror. And so the boy realized several hitherto unsuspected things that would poison his school days. His name was a veritable tangle of animal words: *chat, chameau, oiseau, os*—cat and camel, bird and bone. As if that were not enough, he was hobbled by his way of tripping words off the tip of his tongue, so that he sucked on the hardest syllables and mushed up the others. This transformed his name into a gummy item of high comedy that crowned his humiliation. The Teacher (what luck!) pressed him no further: *I am most grrateful to you for allowing me to glimpse your august person, dear sir* . . .

"Piesent!"

"Nay!"

"Pesent!"

"Nada!"

"Present!"

"Ah."

But there was worse. Continuing through the roll, the Teacher pronounced a name that drew no reaction. He repeated it two or three times with no more success. He completed the list and then, seized with doubt, asked if anyone had not been called. The little boy's immediate neighbor on the bench rose in shaky hesitation.

"Me, *mêssié* . . ."

"And what is your last name, young man?"

"Big Bellybutton, *mêssié* . . ."

"Excuse me?"

"Big Bellybutton, *mêssié* . . ."

The Teacher approached him with languid menace. He searched for evidence of cheekiness. But all he saw was a frightened child.

"This, I prresume, is what you are called at home and in the woods around your shack?"

"Huh?"

"Come with me this instant . . ."

And, intent on scrupulous verification of identity, he led off to the principal's office the ignorant little fellow who answered only to his Creole nickname.*

In the Teacher's absence, the class remains silent. Few rascals dare make a sound. Everyone breathes easier and takes a good

*Répondeurs: [Translator:

Non Bwa-mitan   Backwoods name

Non Savann   Savanna name

Non neg-soubawou   Field-nigger name

Non Kongo!   Darky name!]

look around. Big chipped blackboard in three panels. Tacked up above it, a couple of pictures of winter scenes. A desk on which sit two or three registers. A cupboard. Hanging in one corner are large, mysterious maps of a country shaped like a hexagon.

Répondeurs:
Dribble-drizzle and gray day.
Chill wind . . .

My first Teacher . . . What did you look like? You were quite dark-skinned; very thin, too; hair smoothed flat with vaseline; a huge Adam's apple that bobbed up and down. What was your name? All that is lost amid a vast panic. This first day of school has shriveled up into emotions themselves confused with those of subsequent first days, from year to year, in classrooms on ever-higher floors in the big old building. First-grade Teacher, you will embody all your colleagues. Men cut from the same cloth. And that first class already contained within itself the pattern for those that followed. It's settled, then: I'm telescoping time, and the schoolhouse floors. Dribble-drizzle and gray day. The same chill wind. Any objection? . . .

The little boy spent the morning like a potato bug under a bitter leaf. He never dared to look directly at the Teacher. This was a stratagem much favored by the small fry. If ever your eyes met, he might suddenly feel like asking you one of his impossible questions. While in his getting-acquainted phase, he paced back and forth, talking, talking, providing information of which his little troop (except, perhaps, for a few of us who were naturally gifted at this sort of thing) could make neither head nor tail. Sometimes he stopped in front of the first rows, trying to catch some furtive eye. At the door, he would gaze out at the silent playground now abruptly filled with his voice, then whirl around to stride back across the room. Suddenly, he advanced down the center aisle. Half huddled beneath his bench, gaze glued to the floor, the little boy listened in dismay as the voice drew closer. After a moment's hush, an iron hand jiggled his shoulder: *Sit up strraight, my frriend, mind your posture, for goodness' sake* . . . Back at the blackboard, the Teacher snatched up the chalk and began the ritual that would from now on set the tempo of endless hours of school: *Who can tell me what day, of what month, of what year it is?*

A thoughtful silence fell.

The little boy had never considered the world from that angle. He knew about church days, Mam Ninotte's washdays, All Saints' Day, Christmas Day, New Year's Day . . . Life was given its rhythm by sunshine or rainy weather, by redfish season and whitefish time . . . and Mam Salinière had never asked that kind of question. One little squirt in the front row stood up, however, and reeled off the day-month-year, earning incomprehensible congratulations from the Teacher (*O gleam of humanity in an ocean of barrbarrism!*), who wrote the answer in a fine hand on the blackboard. It was a Monday. In the month of September. In the devil only knows what year.

"I drraw your attention, gentlemen, to what I have just wrritten. Do you not observe a certain elegance in the way these lines grrow sometimes fat and sometimes slender? Is this not so? . . . For your inforrmation, these are called upstrrokes and downstrrokes. No wrriting without upstrrokes and downstrrokes . . ."

The little boy's life was saved by the bell. From that day forward he would learn to welcome it with a deep, invigorating breath. This ringing set off a terrific din upstairs — you could just feel the classrooms explode. The stairwells filled with liberated hordes, and after a slight, pregnant pause, pandemonium would erupt into the courtyard.

Time for recess . . .

Some dummy had the misfortune to pop right up out of his seat. The Teacher pounced on him like a red wasp: *Who told you to rrise? Are you in charge here? Sit, scoundrrel, good-for-nothing, budding wrretch, diminutive scalawag of a rrap-scallion!* They were stunned to learn that, captain of his ship by divine right, the Teacher ran absolutely everything. He and he alone gave permission to stand up. To sit down. To open one's mouth. When he spoke, all eyes and ears were to be trained on him. Pay attention, look alive, and sit up straight. The Teacher was to be spared any bunny-mumbles, any bovine, sun-drowsy yawns, any stupid-ass-molasses-lapping grins, any barnyard cackles from beneath the desks. All bladders — and the neighboring tubes — were to be emptied before entering this sanctuary, thus obviating the need to ask anything that did not pertain to pure knowledge. A raised finger was to be the outward and visible sign of a flash of intelligence rather than the always irritating announcement of a scatological emergency. Not even a fly should buzz without permission. After class had begun, no one should have anything more to say — not to himself, not to the devil or the Goodlord, and absolutely not to his neighbor.

"A classroom is not a bedlam, gentlemen! Order! Discipline! Rrespect! Now, the first rrow will rrise and file out silently, in an orderly and disciplined fashion. Good. Now the second rrow . . ."

Thenceforward the sound of the bell produced nothing more in them than an irrepressible shudder of pleasure, which they had to learn to conceal from the Teacher's newly watchful eye.

Out on the playground, the little boy found himself instantly surrounded by several bullies (probably embittered pupils repeating first grade because of their awkwardness at reading *B-a-Ba*) who ran through the list of animals in his name, while other rough boys made fun of his lisp. He could see that his usual defenses would not work here: going stiff-as-a-stone, flopping to the ground in tears, twitching with the ague, looking woebegone — nothing doing. So he spat at them. Ptooey! The frisky monsters dodged his spit gobs. They barred his way in front, they blocked him off behind, they capered in a circle around him when he stood stock still. Hard pressed, the little boy was at a total loss. His breath came in shuddering gasps, his shoulders shook, his heavy heart beat painfully within his heaving breast. He was overwhelmed with shame. Then bang — the pack swooped down on Big Bellybutton, the child who hadn't known his own name. The little boy watched the poor devil take off at bird speed, pursued by a string of bullies in seventh heaven.

Taking advantage of this diversion, the little boy went looking for Paul. He knew his brother was in one of the upstairs classes, and he planned to seek refuge with him against the eventual return of his tormentors. Spotting Paul through the whirl of older students (the new kids were still clumped before their classrooms or standing with their backs to the wall, trying to assess the dangers of this world), he darted toward him. Paul, completely absorbed in his game, turned — unfortunately — just as his brother ran up to him. Bonk! The collision was inevitable. The smaller boy saw swarms of fireflies. Paul wound up flat on his back with a lump on his forehead, limbs every which way, cursing that mole cricket who dogged his steps even on the playground. As for the little boy, he was brave enough not to cry, and pressing a hand over his bruise, he slipped away into the sportive throng before a scornful crowd could gather. A few observant fiends were already pointing at them and shouting nasty things. He spent the rest of his first recess near a row of faucets at which the children sucked relentlessly, as though they'd never seen such a thing before.

Big Bellybutton was still on the run. Every so often the little guy would stop, raise a fist the size of an egg, bare his milk teeth, spit, and try to hide in a corner of the yard . . . *Awa!* The pack stayed right on his heels. *I pa konnèt non'y! . . . I pa konnèt non'y! . . . Doesn't know his own name!* They pushed him. They snatched at him. They shredded him. They plucked him. They minced him. They tripped him. They pinched and tweaked him. They pulled him around by his shirttail. While he was picking up a torn-off button, they knocked him over and sent him tumbling like a soccer ball. All this was drowned out by the general hullabaloo. And so the little boy realized that the playground was a pitiless place of all-out warfare, something like a jungle or a desert, where mass murder could be committed without anyone even noticing. With sudden inspiration, Big Bellybutton took shelter beneath the low roof that covered part of the courtyard, where the Teachers were gathered. The mob evaporated like misty rain on a parched field.

Where are my *Répondeurs*?

Under the roof, the Teachers were talking among themselves. Now and then they would take a step outside their personal domain to break up a fight, slow down a child barreling along too fast, pick up a tot sent flying by a Big Kid. The Teachers wore trousers, vests, jackets, and ties. They walked like senators. They never turned just their heads, always their entire bodies. Their gestures were restrained and seemed intended to give silken wings to their words. When approached by Monsieur le Directeur (a man of their ilk but with a sterner look, gray hair, hands clasped behind his back, shoulders bowed beneath the combined burdens of wisdom and worry), they bowed before him as if in church and, unctuously respectful, hung on his every word. His presence galvanized the Teachers, who then began to keep a closer eye on the children, to venture out into the yard, to dispense advice, to raise an admonitory finger at anyone who forgot to turn off a faucet. Not one of them noticed Big Bellybutton trembling in their protective shadow.

Monsieur le Directeur did not often appear during recess; his arrival usually meant that the bell was about to ring. His eye was all-seeing. He noticed dripping faucets, half-open doors on the toilet stalls, children running around with forbidden treasures—a comic book, a marble, a slingshot . . . He scurried about like a fire ant, busy with emergencies that only he could discern and that vanished as soon as he'd hustled off.

Monsieur le Directeur never spoke to the children except in reprimand. He was not one for *hello*s and *how-are-you*s. He did not look at anyone but would glare witheringly at any insolent boy who forgot to greet him or at a wild-child too lost in frenzy to notice his approach. With Monsieur le Directeur, the little boy took some measure of the trap into

which he had crammed himself. The children spoke among themselves in shrill voices, with their own words, using their native ways and expressions. The advance of Monsieur le Directeur across the playground caused abrupt freeze frames all around him. Runners stopped running. Jumpers stopped jumping. Chatterboxes stopped chattering. Speechifiers practically swallowed their tongues. He more or less anesthetized all life. Those who thus modified their behavior were old hands at this, from the classrooms upstairs.

But not everybody quieted down.

One little live wire, a greenhorn, did not see Monsieur le Directeur coming. He was yammering away about some old neighbor-lady who could change into a flying sorceress. Hunched over all twisty-faced and waving his arms around, the Storyteller was still pouring out his tale when Monsieur le Directeur arrived. Other oblivious children were listening open-mouthed in a compact circle, fired up by the story. Grasping the Creature by the ear, Monsieur le Directeur dragged him hither and thither: *What do I hear — you're speaking Creole? And what do I see — shameless monkeyshines? Just where do you think you are?! Speak properly and behave in a civilized manner . . .* All the young newcomers took serious note. The passage of Monsieur le Directeur was strewn with cemetery statues.

The little boy never became one of those playground lightning bolts that streaked pell-mell through the yard, hide-and-seeking, fisticuffing, whirly-dervishing like rats in a demijohn. He would sit off in a corner talking with some other kid like himself. Once in a long while he could be seen racing around like a headless chicken, helter-skeltering. But such episodes were rare. And out of character. His nature was contemplative. He watched the others, observed their frights, their joys, their angers, identified the good guys and the bad guys, the savages and gentle souls. Sometimes he wandered over to the front gate, where a candy lady (*O majesty! . . . Answer me . . .*) sold coconut sweeties, sugar twists, peanut caramels, tamarind comfits, lots of confections he could hardly ever buy because Mam Ninotte didn't give him any money. During that first recess, Mam Ninotte appeared at the gate. The little boy ran to her like a madman, ready to wriggle through the bars. He could already see himself, homeward bound. But she explained to him that school wasn't over yet and handed him a *pain au chocolat*. A pure marvel that he chewed on sadly, watching her disappear along the enticing streets of Downtown.

Répondeurs:
Candy Lady
treasure trove
store of happiness
no wrinkle or skinflintiness
no bitter pennypinching
could tell against
the splendors of your tray
O majesty!
O sugarplum!

The bell.

The uproar ceased — flap! — and the children lined up double file by classes in front of the row of Teachers. Monsieur le Directeur observed these maneuvers from a distance, waiting for the correct degree of quiet. Waiting. Waiting. Seeing that the requisite hush was long in coming, Monsieur le Directeur frowned his way between the rows of pupils, casting a cold eye on those still horsing around, while the Teachers verified the straightness of each line and checked to see that all partners were holding hands. Waiting. Waiting. Then the waves of happiness receded, stranding the small fry. All energy ebbed from their muscles. All expression drained from their faces. In a spectral silence, Monsieur le Directeur pushed the button of the electric bell. The upstairs classes rippled into motion like tame caterpillars, followed by the ground-floor pupils. Back in his classroom, the little boy found his asphyxia waiting for him right where he had left it.

But everything went well: no one had to speak, to write, to explain this-or-that. It was the Teacher who talked. And now the little boy realized something obvious: *the Teacher spoke French*. Mam Ninotte used snippets of French on occasion (a half-word here, a quarter-word there), bits of French that were automatic and unchanging. And the Papa, when he made a rum punch, ceremoniously unfurled a French that was less a language than an esoteric tool used for effect. As for the Big Kids, their natural mode of expression was Creole, except with Mam Ninotte, other grownups, and most particularly the Papa. A certain respectful distance was maintained through rituals of formality when speaking to them. And everything else for everyone else (pleasures, shouts, dreams, hatreds, the life in life . . .) was Creole. This division of speech had never struck the little boy before. French (to which he didn't even attach a name) was some object fetched when needed from a kind of shelf, outside oneself, but which sounded natural in the mouth, close to Creole. Close through the articulation. The words. The sentence structure. But now, with the Teacher, speaking traveled far and wide along a single road. And this French road became strangely foreign. The articulation changed. The rhythm changed. The intonation changed. Words that were more or less familiar began to sound different. They seemed to come from a distant horizon and no longer had any affinity with Creole. The Teacher's images, examples, references did not spring from their native country anymore. The Teacher spoke French like the people on the radio or the sailors of the French line. And he deliberately spoke nothing else. French seemed to be the very element of his knowledge. He savored this smooth syrup he secreted so ostentatiously. And his language did not reach out to the children, the way Mam Salinière's had, to envelop, caress, and persuade them. His words floated above them with the magnificence of a ruby-throated hummingbird hovering in the breeze. *Oh, the Teacher was French!*

Répondeurs:
All along the horizon
on a calm sea
use your Creole.
If the weather changes
surging billows
wallowing troughs
gird your loins
get a grip on your French.

Mama, it's hard . . . Baffled, the little black boy realized that he did not know this language. The chatty lil' voice in his head used a different language, his home-language, his Mama-language, the language he had not learned but rather absorbed with ease as he eagerly explored his world. An alien French streaked through this language in flashes that were fleeting and rare; he had heard these words somewhere and he repeated them on occasions he couldn't quite pin down. Another French that was closer to him, acclimated but just as constricted, was lurking on the edge of the living intensity of his mind. But really speaking—to say something, give vent to an emotion, express yourself, think things over, talk for any length of time—required the Mama-tongue that (ayayaye!) was proving useless in school.

And dangerous.

Oh-so-hard! . . .

The Teacher spoke until the noon bell rang. What did he talk about? Undoubtedly the light shed by Wisdom on benighted minds. Doubtless he praised the public school those of his generation had fought so hard to establish. He urged those with the good fortune to be sitting there to appreciate this extraordinary advantage: a golden opportunity, hard-won, not to be wasted. Or else — the cane fields. Sweeping gutters and thumping drums. Lugging sacks of béké goods around the waterfront, raking shellfish from the mudflats of Terres-Sainville, dredging the canals of La Levée. Or worse: winding up in the streets, fettered by ignorance and stupidity. The bestial darkness in which one lost forever the idea of Man.

Time-to-time, he'd stop to see what effect this oration was having on his rapt flock. He searched eyes and faces, hoping to read there glimmers of their inmost feelings. The little boy kept his head down or hurriedly looked away at the Teacher's slightest movement. Several times he felt the latter's gaze directed full upon him and was relieved when the intimidating voice, moving from one end of the blackboard to the other, would continue as though to itself: *State education, gentlemen, public education — it was a harrd battle, and one that is still being fought every day; we were Caesar, Alexander, and Napoleon, warrriors and conquerors shaking all the earrth, and no mountain was high enough to stay the course of our thirrst for knowledge . . .*

O comfort beyond measure: holding your mama's hand after a morning at school! You are all made of joy. Quivering with contentment. Waving bye-bye to the other youngsters, who are escaping just like you. You trot on home as though it were the only place unscathed in a world turned upside-down. And each step away from school is meant to be forever. And no one looks back. Swarming with schoolchildren, Downtown is recalled to life, and you're happy after all to be a part of it: you've grown up just a bit. Less fearful now, you find you're proud of your experience, and you swing your satchel once again like a jaunty altar boy. I speak of the quiet triumph of that homeward journey. *Sweets! Candies, oh!* . . .

The house recovers its former magic. The staircase shadows are once more thronged with seductive spirits. The spider webs shimmer anew with the evanescence of watered silk. The tranquility of the kitchen roof becomes a hideaway where one may contemplate the meaning of life. Everything is dulce. Everything is pleasurable. His spirits soar in a whirl of acclamation.

He takes stock of his familiar world in other ways. He discovers a thousand details. Now he's looking at things he never noticed before. High up on a wall, a picture of Christ suddenly appears: chestnut-brown hair, and blue eyes that move to the left, to the right, watching the little boy. He finally appreciates the fairy-tale scene hanging over Mam Ninotte's bed: near a Chinese junk, undines are bathing in water that's unbelievably green; translucent veils add luster to their pale skin; blond cherubs flutter around them, singing and playing the harp with sublime innocence; on the horizon looms a turreted castle that stabs the mauvish sky with a threat of imprisonment; soft outlines of a forest encircle the misty water invitingly . . . You gaze at this Saturnian idyll, you gaze . . . and gaze . . .

And what about this other one, over the buffet?

Country folk, standing in the twilight, heads bowed, hands clasped, farm tools lying scattered on the ground around an old basket. In the distance, haystacks like rolling hills blend into a solemn sunset pricked by the spire of a church tower . . . a magical hour . . . a reverent depiction of working the land, a scene expressing the abiding power of fate, sorrow, courage, tenderness, hope . . . Mesmerized, the little boy can't stop looking at these pictures. Mam Ninotte had bought them from a Syrian shopkeeper. These images adorned every home in the country at that time—and still do today.

After the midday meal, the little boy saw that the hour approached when Mam Ninotte would sit down at her sewing machine. O moment of happiness! He realized with a pang that he had not fully appreciated this moment until now! He began to wait in blissful anticipation—but his vigil was cut short: *Go put your school clothes back on, it's time to leave!*

And everything is distressing.

The shirt is a corset.

The shoes and socks become agonizing pincers. Inside the once fantastic satchel lurk secret fears. The little boy (who doesn't dare tell Mam Ninotte how unwilling he is to go back there) looks like a wilted flower. His feet drag. The stairs have grown gigantic. His moist hand does not grip Mam Ninotte's; she is the one holding on to him. His tummy's in trouble. His shoes hurt. Is that a feeble cough? But it doesn't move Mam Ninotte to pity—never mind, she says, it's nothing . . .

Répondeurs:
Gird your loins!
Gird your loins!

Survival

Heading off to school in the early afternoon, you encounter skittering dust devils. The Syrians have lowered their rolling metal curtains. The jewelers allow just a peek, through a half-open shutter, at their treasures on display. A tailor still hunches over the lapels of a jacket; with his tape measure tied around his neck, he looks like a fugitive from the gallows. A street vendor (always the same one) is already on her way home, wearily lugging her empty baskets. Blinds stripe the blissful half-light of dining rooms; net curtains soften the tawny gleam of polished mahogany furniture. At the end of dark passageways hovers the luminous image of an earthenware basin, a golden faucet, and a negress ironing flashes of whiteness. Deserted balconies are triumphantly festooned with sun-loving flowers, all screaming out their colors. Facades are lofty, sharp-pointed, implacable. Hot asphalt sweats out a smell of misfortune. At each street corner you run into other anxious schoolchildren, other flinty-hearted mamas. At each corner, you draw closer ... It just keeps getting harder ...

The classroom was familiar and threatening. So was the Teacher. This time, that big old building fell silent very quickly. The Teacher took his place in front of them even more quickly. The playground lay bleaching in the afternoon sun. A listless breeze poked around in the dust. The desks were banded with molten strips of light. Not a breath of air stirred in the room. The youngsters were a mite drowsy, and the little boy began to think longingly of the nap that had always bored him in

Mam Salinière's house. For a moment he hoped the Teacher would announce a heads-down among the inkwells; then he understood that nap time had been banished from this new world. What do the *Répondeurs* have to say?

The first lesson was an exercise in ethics: the Teacher told them a story and asked questions. A poor peasant must feed his family, but his entire fortune consists of a single apple tree. This tree bears dozens of apples. As luck would have it, however, the tree has grown crookedly. Most of the apples dangle gracefully over the street. The poor man picks this fruit regularly to sell at the market, thereby earning enough to buy milk for his children. It is thanks to these apples that his little ones do not starve. But on some spring days, when he goes to his tree, he finds nothing. Not one apple.

What has happened?

Dubitative silence in the classroom.

The Teacher waited awhile, then pointed to a luckless boy.

"You! What do you think happened?"

"Dunno, *mêssié . . .*"

"Someone picked the apples, of courrse! Apples that did not belong to him. In picking these apples, has this perrson, in your opinion, perrforrmed a good deed?"

"Ah nooo, *mêssié . . .*"

"Correct. And this perrson—what should we call him?"

"He's a chicken t'ief, *mêssié . . .*"*

"*Th* . . . ief, not t'ief! Apple thief, not chicken thief! A chicken thief steals chickens, an apple thief steals apples. Is it rright to steal?"

"Nooo!" (Unanimous cry from the audience, which thus managed to take a little breather.)

*In Creole, a pilferer is called a chicken thief, no matter what has been stolen.

"Is it rright to pick frrom a trree that does not belong to us?"

"Nooo!"

Moral: *I will not pick apples that do not belong to me.*

And then he wrote it all out on the blackboard.

At the supper table that evening, the little boy recounted this business about the apple tree, but no one seemed impressed. The Papa merely wondered wherever did he think he could pick apples, since they all had to be imported to the island by boat in closed crates and arrived half rotten ... Unfazed by such incomprehension, the little boy topped off his drawings of their home by adding a bunch of apple trees, red with gigantic fruit, surrounded by policemen wielding huge truncheons.

He also drew tall, pointy castle towers and steeples rising sharply into skies striped with black clouds. He drew a wolf.

On the following day, class began with a different ritual. The Teacher gave an energetic imp the task of filling the inkwells in each desk. The inkwells came alive with a shining, unfathomable liquid full of mystery. The little boy peered into his inkwell as through a window opening onto unknown places. He wanted to stick his finger in it, taste it, get inside it. As compact as the pupil of an eye, the ink rippled whenever he fidgeted on his bench. So he fidgeted. Chalk dust began to settle onto the surface of the ink like a raft in distress. So, puffing discreetly, he blew in more dust from the desk top. Suddenly, through all this staring into the inkwell, he tumbled into a blackish tempest battering flotillas of struggling boats. The waves were ink. The wind was ink. The vessels were sculpted in ink. Sometimes midnight-blue lightning streaked through the scene. He managed to grab hold of an ink raft.

Whack! Whack! He began to flail about in the storm with an inky oar to drive away the ink-monsters surging up from the abyss . . .

Tak! The Teacher's voice broke the spell . . .

Now the Teacher ordered the distribution to each pupil of a penholder, a wooden shaft tipped with a slender nib, which pen was to be left in the groove at the top of each desk and touched only with the Teacher's permission. Then he had exercise books, each bearing a child's name, given out to the entire class. The little boy received his notebook but was unable to inspect it, because there again, it was to be put away in a corner of his desk. The little boy was so exhilarated by these new wonders, within reach yet inaccessible, that he could hear his heart beating with elation.

The days were to slip by like that, gradually domesticating the inkwells, the pens, and the exercise books, which were handed out every morning and handed in every afternoon. They never left the school. They became familiar to us, and with each passing day we would leave a trace of ourselves behind in them. The inkwell will always cherish the opaque memory of time. The pen (its nib soon spoiled and often replaced) will never forget the first downstrokes, the muddy upstrokes, and the notebook of squared paper (ha! I see you, triumphant knight, your steed rearing through all eternity on every cover) will become the bible of our failures, fears, and costly victories. *O heart of today!* Every inkwell, every pen, every blue-lined notebook, anywhere, at any hour, at any age, sets off cindery showers, sandy torrents, billowing smoke, fleeting crumblings—all sweeping in a rush through head and heart . . . and the man I am now (built upon this nothingness) is touched by it as by a private glory.

I can describe what it feels like: the exercise-book covers, in brilliant new colors that flash in the light, soft and rich to the touch, with their unfamiliar plastic smell that permeates the first days of school and clings to the notebooks of dazzling, cross-ruled whiteness . . . And their dull oblivion: torn, ink-stained, their fiery colors silently snuffed out. I well remember that astonishment: *a host of covers ushering in uncertain times* . . .

Répondeurs:
True heart of today!

Our day continued rather inauspiciously, however. The Teacher had the bright idea of verifying the success of his lesson in ethics. This was to be his daily practice. He was moved to call upon Big Bellybutton, who, like the little boy, was attempting to make himself invisible. Big Bellybutton had arrived late. Sweating like a colicky horse, he had just managed to reach the tag end of the column as it marched off to class. By some miracle, Monsieur le Directeur had not spotted him. The Teacher had, though, and had wiggled a finger stiff with disapproval at him. Big Bellybutton thought he'd had a narrow squeak, but as it is never clever to get yourself noticed in such perilous places, he came naturally to mind when the Teacher decided to evaluate the effects of his lecture. When his name was called, Big Bellybutton rose looking like Christ crucified with no miracle in sight.

"What was yesterday's moral?"

"The apples, *mêssié* . . ."

"The apples, the apples . . . and what else?"

A few veterans raised eager hands, itching to reel off the right answer, but the Teacher ignored them and kept his eyes on Big Bellybutton the way a cat watches a mouse hole.

"Mustn't pick apples, *mêssié* . . ."

"Fine. But picking someone else's prroperty without perrmission is called . . . what?"

"That's called apple-stealing, *mêssié . . .*"

"Good."

The Teacher was going to stop there, but alas, while he was there, a vague suspicion came over him.

"Have you ever picked anything without perrmission?"

"Uhhh . . . yes, *mêssié . . .*"

"And what is that called?"

"Dunno, *mêssié . . .*"

"You just told me a second ago, it's called *st . . . st . . .*"

Suddenly, in an absolute lather of bug-eyed terror, fluttering his hands before his sweaty face, Big Bellybutton began to screech, *'Twasn't apples, mêssié, 'twas mangoes, not apples! 'Tisn't stealing, 'tisn't stealing! . . . 'Cause it was mangoes, mêssié!*

The Teacher heaved a poignant sigh . . . but his worries had only begun.

"We shall now study," said the Teacher, "the sound *a. A* is the firrst letter of the alphabet. You may not be familiar with apples, but you will immediately rrecognize what I am about to show you. Its name begins with an *a.*"

Reaching into a bag, he pulled out an *ananas* and carefully placed it on the class register.

"What is this fruit called?" he asked triumphantly, after a lengthy pause for collective identification.

His hands were joined as if in prayer; his head, tilted to one side, seemed to droop slightly in sympathy with his downcast eyes.

A hearty cry burst from the congregation.

"A *zanana, mêssié!*"*

Horrors.

---

*In Creole, *ananas* (pineapple) is pronounced *zanana*. (Note from the Omniscient One.)

The Teacher gulped. His face was contorted with anguish. His eyes became glittering stones. *Zounds! . . . However do you expect to trravel along the path to wisdom with a language like that! This po'-nigger talk gums up your minds with its worrthless pap!* His indignation was absolute. And his compassion as well. He paced furiously about, scanning woebegone faces, searching for the authors of this outrage. Perspiration shone upon his brow and trickled down to sully the whiteness of his collar. He studied us intently, speaking now in sorrow, now in anger, and his voice betrayed the faintest quaver of blighted hopes. Then he seemed to take refuge upon a distant shore, where he wondered just how deeply bogged down in ignorance we were. His outstretched arms invoked the massive cleansing required for the salvation of our fold: *Before these Augean stables, even Herrcules would quail!*

Through lesson after lesson, Hercules labored mightily to drag examples of a few elementary sounds from his herd. For the sound *ou*, they suggested the *manicou* possum, the *balaou* needlefish, the *boutou* truncheon, words that don't exist in French. For *o*, all they offered was *boloko*, a vulgar word for a country lout. When the unfortunate Teacher tried to illustrate the sound *eu* with *feu*, the French word for fire, one harebrained fellow (thinking it meant the Creole punch savored at noon) shouted excitedly that his father made some every day. The Teacher worried that a pyromaniac was on the loose—until he realized that, once again, he had been tripped up by barbarians.

When the children spoke, they had a natural tendency to change every *u* to an *i*. *Juste* became *jiste*; *refusé* degenerated into *refisé*. The sound *eur* slipped into *ère*: *docteur* wound up *doctère*, *fleur* became *flère*, *inspecteur* slid into *inspectère*. But much worse, in the Teacher's opinion, was the disappearance of the *r: force* was reduced to *fôce.* Then the Teacher would go on a rampage of mocking, teasing, scolding, wailing, yelling, frowning, and tapping with his ruler. He closed in on the left, pressed hard on the right, tried to ward off disaster by demonstrating the proper articulation with his own lips as a pupil was speaking or by abruptly cutting short someone who had gotten off to a "bad" start. Sometimes he called the whole class to witness: *Just listen to that brute!* Then a fresh-from-France kid would proudly rise and rattle off the proper accent.

We had only three fresh-from-France boys, but seated up in the front row, they magnetized the class. One of them, the son of a mulatto customs officer who drove a fancy car, had recently arrived on the ship *Colombie.* Ignorant of all things Creole, he displayed a Parisian refinement of behavior, vocabulary, and accent that sent the Teacher into raptures. Neither of the other two (one was a well-to-do doctor's kid and one the son of a wicked tax inspector) had ever traveled beyond the walls of his family fortress, into which the Creole world seemed never to have poked its nose. Their parents had sealed them inside an environment of pictures of France, preventive behavior, supervised pronunciation, closely watched manners; this pair that had turned up on our school benches were thus as exotic as if they had come from the impossible lands that lie behind God's back. They were less self-confident than our junior customs officer but more talented than any of us at adapting to the cultural orthopedics deployed by the Teacher.

Each of us tried hard to keep a watch on himself. The children began to laugh at those who couldn't manage a decent *u* or *r.* Opening your mouth had become a risky business. You had to listen closely to the lil'-mama-tongue wagging in your thoughts, translate everything into French, and prevent your natural pronunciation from spoiling these new sounds. A dreadfully tall order. When the Teacher asked a question, only the smarty-pants-from-France (or those whose parents had made careful French speech a fundamental principle of their lives) were able to reply without gagging on their *u*s and swallowing their *r*s. What I'm saying is, speech became a heroic feat. You were chancing not only a tongue-lashing from the Teacher but also hot pursuit out on the playground by a pack of fiends, even though they weren't any better at French than the rest of us. Their own ineptitude simply made them meaner. *I fè an kawô! I fè an kawô! He made a mistake!* From one day to the next, some unlucky answer or phrase might plunge you into barbarous grotesquerie. Silences deepened as you tiptoed through letters, sounds, words. Each one of us felt worthless.

"What do you see here?"
    "A hoss, *mêssié*!"
    "Egad! It's a horrse!"

"At the end of his fishing line, Papa attaches a . . . a . . . "
    "A sniggle!"
    "No, a fishhook, *isalop*!"

In his frustration, the Teacher himself might relapse into Creole. He would also, in the occasional moment of fatigue, skimp on his *r*s or lose his *u*s. But he'd catch himself in a flash. His wary self-command would then become intense, unremitting, strained to the highest pitch. His flickering language would grow even more painstaking, guarded, distrustful of itself, threading its way among sounds while anticipating hazardous pitfalls where the dreaded Creole lurked near at hand. In his desperate desire to be articulate, he embellished his speech by slathering on the France-white accent, multiplying his *rs*, sticking out his lips as though they were sharp blades meticulously chiseling the sounds tripping from his tongue.

"The capital of Frrance is . . ."

"Paru, *mêssié . . .*"

"Parris, you sorrry prrat! What's the matter with you?! You're perrfectly capable of prronouncing an *i*, after all!"

The youngsters had begun to be suspicious of all *i*s. Certain judicious souls had found it simpler to strike the sound from their vocabulary in favor of a universally upgraded *u*. Bespattered with unbelievable gibberish, the Teacher had to put his foot down to get the *i*s back. Then the children started scattering *rs* around where there weren't any. *Châtier* became *chârtier*, *fumer* became *furmer*. Each child did his anxious best to scrabble up to the summit of knowledge, and everyone floundered around with this over-pronounced French. Now the Teacher hated Creole more than ever, seeing in it the root of these evils, the ball and chain that would keep the children prisoners of ignorance. He called upon our parents to protect their progeny from the contamination of this cane-fields pidgin by demanding that we speak French, the language of wisdom, wit, and intelligence. No Creole under any circumstances, particularly when we children were talking among ourselves. That rank weed was to be immolated on pyres of exemplary vigilance.

Seeing us staggered by this language problem day after day only stiffened the Teacher's resolve. We watched him grapple somberly with our insane difficulties; we felt his despair when the soft singsong of our Creole accents dragged out our drawling, dawdling French. Then he would straighten up, take a deep breath, hitch up his pants with a flap of his elbows, withdraw into himself (and as far away as possible from us), and trusting in God, unleash the splendor of his universal French . . .

Sometimes the Teacher tried to winkle sentences out of the children, but (perplexed by worries inside their heads, where the lil'-mama-tongue was still under house arrest), they all sat mum. The little boy had arrived with a mindful of mysteries—things seen, the bizarre habits of insects, how to understand night-blooming flowers or become one with the wind, toying with the mere dust on a window sill—and he could sense the souls of motionless beings that haunted abandoned temples, the secret sighs that drifted out of tiny chinks in the world. In an effort to spark discussion, the Teacher sometimes showed them pictures, any one of which the little boy could have turned into a thousand words, but the Teacher had reduced him to a silence that only deepened each time he heard the now constant lament: *Oh, this Crreole brrood has nothing to say!*

One day, the Teacher brought in a tamarind branch stripped of leaves and hung it up over the blackboard. Whoever skidded into a Creole word or errant turn of phrase earned himself a stinging swat on the legs. The switch began to prey on everyone's mind. The little boy grew even more mouse-quiet. His tongue soon seemed heavy to him, his speech too slurred, his accent hateful. His little inner voice grew ashamed; his natural chattiness deteriorated into an illicit activity to be stifled in the presence of Big Kids and shouted among other small fry to make up for it. Among themselves, the youngsters did not speak French. First of all, because Creole was their native tongue, and besides, French had become risky there as well. Whoever called a newspaper a *jounal* instead of a *journal* was branded for life. The slightest taint of Creole set off a merciless festival of mockery. It was all or nothing in French. As for

Creole, it circulated easily but in a dilapidated state. Degraded to contraband, it grew callous from its freight of insults, dirty words, hatreds, violence, and tales of catastrophe. Creole wasn't used anymore to say nice things. Or loving things, either. It became the language of bad guys, thugs, and delinquent crazy-buggers. Vulgar Creole was the sign of crudeness and violence. The little boy's linguistic equilibrium was turned topsy-turvy. Forever.

"What do you see here?"
   "A stewpot!"
   "Heavens, no—it's a skillet!"

"Here now, what's this about a zombie?! Haven't you ever hearrd of elves, gnomes, fairries, and will-o'-the-wisps? Spare me your *soucougnans* and three-leg-horses!"

Teacher's despair: the children spoke through images and meanings they took from Creole. A newcomer was *fresh off the boat*; *wicked* meant *extraordinary*; a slanderer was a *bad-mouther*; a crossroads was a *four-way*; a weakling was called a *droopy-dick*; when something was sad you called it *chimerical*; to start involuntarily became *to seize up*; an uproar was a *foofaraw*; a conflict was a *tear-up*—and so on. Stars shone like snake eyes, avocado skins, or *kouli* hair. A person was as beautiful as a coral tree in May, and everything ugly was old ... Whenever a youngster opened his mouth, the Teacher seemed to hear (he claimed, aghast) the howling of a wolf ... *zero, ze-ro, zee-rro!*

"Petit-Pierre gobbles so many mulberries out in the village fields that he gives himself a violent stomachache. You might call him a glut ..."

"Agoulou . . ."
"Who said that?! Who said that?!"

During recess, Big Bellybutton shook off his tormentors, who found themselves an unexpected victim: an unfortunate Big Kid in the queerest getup. Perhaps he had committed some piece of foolishness or other. The Teacher must have sent a note home to the parents, because early the next morning the poor thing had been sent to school in a flour sack with holes cut out for his head and arms. His appearance in the courtyard triggered vast hilarity. The youngest children began to go wild all around him, and Big Bellybutton was the first in line. The Big Kid couldn't do a thing but go deaf and blind and never notice the pushes and trip-ups coming in from all sides. He had nowhere to turn to. Since the courtyard shelter was out of the question (the Teachers there were wearing faces of severest disapproval), he wandered about the playground, chevied by a pack that would cry off only with the bell. Time-to-time, the exasperated offender would try to throttle one of his tormentors. Then the circle would explode, leaving our man spinning like a wooden top, his contortions made even clumsier by the infamous sack flapping at his knees.

"You shouldn't say *mama*—the word is pronounced *ma-mah*, you hear me, you scamps?!"

In days to come, the little boy would see many of these unhappy children pilloried by their parents for misbehaving in school. Some of them showed up sporting bald spots clipped by hostile scissors. Others had to keep wearing trousers they had torn, with rips that put their butt-cheeks on display. Anyone caught chewing some Malabar by a Teacher would have to explain to his parents why he'd come home wearing bubblegum in his hair. Others wore signs they'd been made to write out themselves: *I am an ass.* But there was worse . . .

"Ye gods in heaven! You shouldn't say, *She's my grammy-nana-nyah-nyah-nyah!* You say, *She's my grrandmother!* Or else, *She's my grranny!* What am I going to do with these nincompoops?

The Teacher was armed. As we blundered along, he unveiled his arsenal. Of course there was the green tamarind switch drying up over the blackboard and renewed from week to week when it wore out or simply vanished, no one knew how. It was flexible and would curve around to nip—tiak!—the back of your leg. The very tip knew how to raise a welt. Sometimes (when he'd been out for a Sunday stroll in the Jardin de Balata, in the hills above Fort-de-France), he brought in a replacement stalk of golden bamboo that struck harshly but soon split open from end to end. In an emergency, he might brandish a length of mango wood picked out on his way to school, another supple switch, but one with a rough surface that empurpled skin as if it were a jellyfish tentacle. He was known to use a stick of mahoe, quite prone to drying out, and in some hour of dark despair he wielded a rod of *ti-baume*, hard as iron and close to bloodthirsty. He occasionally brought us a calabash liana harvested at peak maturity, a furious biter and flat-out indestructible. I also remember the volcano-wood switch (he called it German vine, because it was invasive) that he could snap above our anguished labors like a gunshot.

When in the mood to refine his method, the Teacher would tell one of us to bring in a switch of his own choosing. The Unlucky One would have to present his find the next day and stand there while the Teacher examined it, gave its Latin name, tested its flexibility, described its afflictive potential, and depending on its apparent sturdiness, voiced his high or low opinion of the stick. That's how Big Bellybutton (who possessed arcane expertise in the plant kingdom) came to be congratulated for a long, greenish harpy, as supple as braided leather, fetched from deep in the woods. The Teacher could neither recognize it nor put a name to it. With downcast eyes that betokened ulterior motives, Big Bellybutton listened so impassively to this uncustomary deluge of felicitations that the Teacher declared him incapable of appreciating rarefied hymns of praise. The seemingly invincible Enigma was draped decoratively above the blackboard, where it intimidated us with the combined menace of the Eye of God and the Sword of Damocles. The Teacher, on the other hand, was exhilarated. You could sense his eagerness to pounce at the first blunder, to sniff out some lurking Creole idiocy; indeed, he questioned the usual lamebrains, hovered alertly near the well-known dullards, baited the wisecrackers and the fraidy-cats. The troop, dug in beneath a *molocoye* tortoise shell, exhibited all the get-up-and-go of a graveyard. The Teacher had to wait two whole days before some slip-up caught his eye and sent him racing to that promising vine. *Awa!* The Invincible broke like a straw on the leg in question—yes, most unexpectedly— yes, at the first blow—yes, without doing diddly. In the matter of switches, the Teacher never bothered Big Bellybutton again.

The Teacher gave names to his switches: there were Durandal, Excalibur, Quicklime, the Snake, Attila, Apocalypse, the Great War, Hiroshima, Joan of Arc, Du Guesclin, the Electric Eel, Robespierre, not counting the Slicers, Stingers, and Tinglers baptized at short notice when he was off his form.

Répondeurs:
The Teachers, armed.

UNIVERSITY OF GLAMORGAN
G
PRIFYSGOL MORGANNWG
Learning Resources Centre

engraved the Body Politic
in stigmata on little legs
thin-skinned memory
scrolls of scars
ho fossil pains and woes
tibias dare to dream

Depending upon the mood and the moment, numerous stages preceded recourse to the whip. You might be told to remain standing at your seat, or behind the blackboard, or facing the wall at the back of the classroom. You might be hoisted up by your ear until you cried mercy for fear it would rip off. Your noggin might receive the devastating thwack of a thumping forefinger. You might be pinched on the shoulder, on the back, grabbed by your belly-skin and dragged up to the blackboard like a baby goat in a Hindu sacrifice. You might . . .

But it wasn't long at all before there were new developments. Whoever was caught gossiping with his neighbor or proved unable to repeat what the Teacher had just said was obliged to go up to the blackboard, hold out his hands, and receive without flinching four or five blows from a ruler on his fingertips, held all bunched together. The switches lost a smidgen of their horror in comparison with this new torture. Another day, he came up with an unprecedented tightening of the screw for those whose heads were on the dense side. Big Bellybutton quickly found himself kneeling in front of the door, forced to clap his fists over his head until the Teacher allowed him to stop. The Teacher forgot about him, of course, and we watched all morning long as his arms moved more and more slowly, then stiffly, then hesitantly, until he fell forward and splatted like a ripe breadfruit. With the pitiless Teacher screaming at him, *And did I tell you to stop, you disobedient sneak?!* The Teacher was armed.

One day, the little boy—like Big Bellybutton and many another—wound up on his knees before the door. Having in the meantime perfected his system, the Teacher had given him two rocks to knock together, tok tok tok, above his head. This punishment had more or less lost its sting; those thus chastised served their time patiently, especially since they were fairly certain of coming out alive. But they hadn't yet understood the hidden peril of this snare. It was not for nothing that the Teacher required the offender to kneel right at the door. The little boy, to his cost, soon found out why . . .

There he was, tok tok tok, sadly smacking those galling rocks, when a light step made his heart sink. Monsieur le Directeur's inspection tours of the building were rather rare, but not as rare as all that. We would learn how to detect this presence floating furtively on a thread of submarine silence, shooting a torpedo look through a window, checking the blackboard, evaluating the Teacher, appraising the students. Sometimes, parked just outside the classroom door, he would nod to the Teacher with a *Please continue*. The Teacher's voice would then ratchet up a notch, his French would grow tauter, and his backbone would stiffen with an extra jolt of steely authority. Standing in the doorway, Monsieur le Directeur would stare at us, whittling us down, and when he moved on, he left behind little shavers burnt to ashes by his flamethrower eyes. We'd see him peeking ever so discreetly around a door jamb. We learned to distinguish the sharp squeak of his patent-leather shoes on the silent stairs. We came to recognize his way of shaking the front gate to make sure it was properly secured. We learned to watch from our seats as he went along the row of water faucets, obstinately twisting the handles down tighter. We found we had to remain on the alert even when the Teacher's back was turned, because Monsieur le Directeur could catch you in a jamboree by suddenly material-

izing at the window . . . and then the sky would come crashing
down on you. In the sunlight, his hair seemed like solid silver.
In the shade, cotton wool with a yellowish tinge. He wore the
same face everywhere, a face of noble gravity, lined and care-
worn, a commanding face. No one ever grew used to seeing
him or encountering him during recess; it was always a heart-
stopper, always a scared-stiffer, always a plunge into primor-
dial guilt that was over your head in a flash, because of the
look in his eyes.

Répondeurs:
Fer!

Monsieur le Directeur, I speak of your silences, your bearing,
your neatness that was proof against all perspiration in spite
of the sun's hammering; I will also recall here your attitude
toward school, toward others, toward life, an attitude forged
in solemn ceremonies familiar to those who once built cathe-
drals. Nigger, you fled from yourself and, with stubborn determination, held your head up high—above the cane fields,
the sugar, the watermelon grins, the *békés*, the dancing, the
drums, the torrents of rum, that life directed entirely toward
sticking us forever in the mud. You loom large over a host of
memories, a tutelary figure. Tutelary, and affecting.

Seeing the little boy kneeling outside the classroom door sent
Monsieur le Directeur into boundless fury. *What are you doing
there, you scapegrace?* And he latched on to the child's ear,
hauled him to his feet, gave him a shove toward the staircase.
Go wait for me in my office . . .

"Who can constrruct a sentence for me to illustrrate the arrival of sprring by evoking a flight of swallows over the snow-
capped church tower of your village? No one? Grracious me!"

The little boy had never climbed those stairs. He knew that Monsieur le Directeur's office was on the top floor, to the left of the last landing. So he started up those deserted steps in a state that doesn't bear telling. Through an open window on the first floor he could see the cheerful hurry-flurry of the street, the still enticing sunshine, the passersby free to roam wherever they pleased, the shops inviting customers in to browse. Everything outside was calling to him. With each step, his shoulders drooped a little lower. When he reached the third floor, he felt sick and wanted to dash back downstairs to hide somewhere. The office door was open. Had he been able to read, he would have understood the sign hanging over the door: *Directeur*. The little boy just stood there and, like a wounded animal, began to wait. There wasn't a single fidget left in him; he even welcomed this suspension of time by freezing into a cataleptic immobility.

A slow footstep echoed up the stairs . . . Monsieur le Directeur appeared. His severity was absolute, unruffled, flawless. He questioned the little boy, who couldn't muster the strength to answer or even hear him. *Why were you punished? Are you going to answer me? So, it seems you've come here to stir up trouble, then!* And he fetched from his cupboard a sophisticated whip, straw colored, ending in a braided thong. The child had to raise his arms over his head, lean against the wall with his legs spread, and receive two whacks on his calves. At the time, happy to hear that he could return to his class, he did not feel much. But as he left the office of Monsieur le Directeur and made his way back downstairs, he was overcome by stinging pain, shame, and misery. He felt broken beyond repair, banished from the world of the living and condemned to drag his bewilderment through a labyrinth of deserted stairways. He was nothing but a limp rag by the time he somehow managed to reach the classroom, only to be sent to his seat by the Teacher without one flicker of compassion. When he slunk down the aisle, the youngsters gaped at him as though he were a Friday-the-thirteenth zombie, fresh from the grave. No one misbehaved for absolutely the longest time. Well, for however long it takes kids to forget sheer horror . . . Oh, answer me . . .

No one ever found out that he'd been punished, and especially not Mam Ninotte. For a couple of days, he worried and worried that the Teacher would complain about him to her when she appeared during morning recess with a *pain au chocolat* for her youngest. Still, how sweet it was to watch her arrive! To see her eyes again, her smile, her body, to feel he was still linked to the world through her, for she was so strong, and she knew so very much about life! How his heart leaped to see her! . . . And yet, areas inaccessible to Mam Ninotte were piling up inside him. He'd begun hiding from her all his unavowable fears, his ignominious anxieties, those sorrows unlikely to earn him an extra dollop of affection. He kept his failures secret, along with the scoldings and the wallops, because Mam Ninotte seemed to confer supreme authority upon the school. She tended to the scholarly requirements of her children with such loving care that you'd have thought it was her sole purpose in life. Grumbling about school to her would have released a flash flood of disapproval. So the little boy's mind began to focus on the idea of surviving the hardships of school.

Surviving.

Getting through it.

And that, he could tell, was estranging him from his family by opening pockets of solitude in the core of his being. In order to keep his new secrets, he cast off subtle ties to the world and made himself opaque to Mam Ninotte. No longer trusting and open with others, he fluttered his lashes over the treacherous innocence of his eyes, learning to leave some space between what his heart felt and what his mouth said. It meant surviving, I say, and dying at the same time.

Encountering Monsieur le Directeur was like experiencing the stinging whiplash—so precise, so exact—all over again. The terror of those empty stairways would surge through him as well. Monsieur le Directeur became the dragon crouched somewhere high above, who could swoop down on you like a cannibal god.

Répondeurs:
Fer!

Sometimes, it's fun: a yellow butterfly wanders into the classroom and does its silly fan dance over the Teacher's head. Or it could be a damselfly, or perhaps a honeybee. One frightful day it's a *mabouya* lizard that darts from a shadowy niche, pursued by who knows what nightmare, and decides to take a stroll across the blackboard. Result: pandemonium. The youngsters, under so much pressure to behave, use these irruptions to let off shrieks of joy and counterfeit fear, a real shivaree, while the Teacher looks on more or less helplessly. *Come now, gentlemen, there's no call for a Racinian tragedy . . . or a Greek one, either . . .*

The little boy's thoughts began to flit about. Whenever he found himself rooted to his seat, irresistible fancies would take flight within him as though to make up for the abnormal immobilization of his body. He himself was unaware of these flutters, for the mind takes off without warning, in the downy stillness of a ghost ship. The Teacher's voice drones on, the classroom fades away—but not entirely; images drift by: Mam

Ninotte, something at home, a fleeting emotion . . . Then the class takes on a shimmering reality once more, only to melt away again. A word, a story, a perplexing phrase stir up endless eddies of fantasy, as though his contact with the world could only jog along in tandem with his dreams. This flickering stardust must have given a marshy sheen to his eye and a hint of slackness to his jaw, because the Teacher eventually caught on to him. *Oh là, our Cyrano de Bergerac is hiding out on the moon again!*

Big Bellybutton, now, he wasn't a daydreamer. He had to be working his hands: he'd scrape at his desk, scratch his feet, rub his nose, twist onto one buttock, then the other, as though his constrained body required a swarm of tactile sensations to participate in the world. He loved to fiddle with chalk, slates, pens, and was constantly flipping notebooks open and closed. He was a little guy with blue-black skin, sharp eyes, hair scorched rusty-red and frazzled by the sun, a body that was already tough and muscular. Having pegged him from the start as the class dunce, the Teacher often used him to illustrate the evils of ignorance. He would casually ask the boy the stickiest, trickiest questions and never failed to thump him with that forefinger when he hazarded an answer. Big Bellybutton was the little boy's shield. Since they shared the same bench, Big Bellybutton drew all the inevitable gibes shot off by the Teacher from the blackboard or the massed scorn of the other children. Sitting next to him, the little boy didn't share this general mocking attitude. He could see the energy in Big Bellybutton's hands, his secret determination to survive, the wariness in his eyes (a vigilance he knew how to conceal), the firm set of his mouth, and the strength of that body mobilized to read the mood of the class, withstand assaults, deflect attention, lie low, keep calm, and soak up his surroundings in school the way an imprisoned wild animal would have done to help prepare his attack. And above all, the little boy saw that Big Bellybutton hadn't lost his ability to smile, which showed his benchmate (who was touched to the heart) how secure he was in the core of his being.

Grownups were the guardians of the world, protective jailers.

In fact, Big Bellybutton surprised us all when the Teacher broached the subject of numbers and calculation. To begin with, he was the first of us to be able to count to ten, even though it was always a struggle for him to write the numbers on his slate. But where he was really unbeatable was doing figures in his head.

The Teacher had brought in a few plastic apples, with which he undertook to reveal to us the joys of arithmetic. Counting from one to ten, then by tens, then by fives, by twos, from one to a hundred . . . etc. Adding, subtracting, dividing . . . when those notions were at last — after great pains — a bit less strange to us, the brilliance of Big Bellybutton shone out, first in brief sparks, then in a dazzling radiance. Calculations involving apples bought sold given shared, pears lost one by one then recovered in threes, trains losing passengers from station to station — all a snap for Big Bellybutton. His hands would roam over the desk, wrap around his knees, pluck at his tummy; his skin would twitch like a grasshopper's antennae, his eyes flash with a stellar fire, and thanks to this carnal alchemy, he'd have found the answer in a trice while the little boy was still wondering what the dickens a train of passengers might be and just what a pear looked like. When the Teacher abandoned the blackboard to launch surprise attacks, the Big Bellybutton phenomenon became even more spectacular.

"I add this to that and I have how many, quick, quick? Then I take away this one, come on, quickly—who can answer? Then I have all this and I give half away, so what's left?"

"Three, *mêssié*."

At first the Teacher thought it was just luck, the kind that turns grubby caterpillars into butterflies. In an effort to cram Big Bellybutton back into his place, the Teacher upped the ante.

"Fine—I've got ten strawberries, I add four and then give seven of them to Humpty-Dumpty; on the way to visit the Three Little Pigs, I lose two of them, so just what do I have left?"

And Big Bellybutton blurts out, "Five!"

Jaws dropped.

The Teacher stood there all flabberdegasky. Unnerved by his own audacity, Big Bellybutton retreated behind his sooty facade and, shrinking himself up, managed to half disappear behind his desk.

Even the Teacher's fancy-mouthed favorites were left in the dust by the whizzing gears in Big Bellybutton's head. The Teacher considered him distrustfully, because that gift for figures didn't jibe with all the rest, with his hayseed air, his blackblackblack skin, his kinky wool, his flat nose, his Creole accent, his complete ignorance of French vocabulary, his chronic tardiness, his sweats . . . It simply didn't make sense. The Teacher decided not to call on him and, under the pretext of letting others have their turn (*Not the same ones all the time, we can't have that!*), imposed on Big Bellybutton a silence that drove the child to a frenetic display of mute wriggling. In any case, the Teacher always seemed more attuned to the intricacies of French than to the vulgar science of numbers, and he gave the impression of presenting that part of his curriculum with only incidental interest. Big Bellybutton's supremacy in the subject reinforced his distaste. *Our frriend is obviously lacking in the spirrit of finesse!* he would exclaim, and in French, reading, writing, vocabulary, he continued to hound the child. To defeat him.

It didn't take the little boy long to notice that the Teacher had his pets. These possessed light skin and fluffy hair that bobbed on their foreheads or waved in lustrous beauty. Their noses weren't wide or flat but long, pointy, and pinched all down their length, as though constantly fending off bad smells. They could already speak a sleek little French they'd acquired from living abroad or from parents with considerable experience in the language. They had nothing to do with what the Teacher called ol'-nigger ways, customs that were actually of Creole origin. Whether he was aware of it or not, the Teacher associated dark skin and Negroid features (even though he had them) with the same no-account world that had produced the Creole culture: each barbarous element implied the other. That was why he shied away from recognizing Big Bellybutton's abilities, while endowing his favorites with a particular aptitude for learning. The Teacher was less severe with his pets. When they gave foolish answers, he wouldn't throw a fit but instead repeated the question for them with adamantine patience, because they simply hadn't heard it correctly, that's all ... When he had to scold them, he never used wounding words, never reached for Durandal or Du Guesclin. The Teacher had his pets.

They were the ones who filled the inkwells, erased the blackboard, dashed off to Monsieur le Directeur's office when the chalk ran out or we had to return a map, a compass, a magnifying glass. They were the ones who distributed the exercise books, pens, textbooks, and collected them again. When they raised a hand, the Teacher would warble in ecstasy, *Ah no not you, not always the same ones*, and start looking for some poor clod. The Teacher had his pets.

The Teachers' pets resembled one another. They kept almost the same distance from us as the Teachers did. They were better dressed, their shoes were finer, their embroidered socks swallowed up their knees. During recess, instead of joining our parched scuffling around the water faucets, they sucked on sugary elixirs carried in showy gourds that hung on their leather belts, driving everyone else to thirsty despair. When a gang of bullies would try to drink from these canteens, their owners could openly seek protection under the Teachers' wings and tell on their tormentors in limpid French. An accusation in French would unleash more devastating reprisals than even the most dramatic Creole complaints. As a result, a Teacher's pet was never harassed.

Big Bellybutton, on the other hand, was still fair game. The little boy watched him turn into a hunted *manicou* possum as soon as the class had scattered across the playground. His persecutors would begin by quenching their thirst at the faucets and chatting for a minute or two, giving the Teachers time to gather in their usual spot. Then the gang would sniff out its victim and descend upon him like a swarm of mosquitoes. Of course Big Bellybutton would remain safely close to the Teachers for as long as possible, but thirst, the itch to run, to give free rein to his demanding body, would drive him into hostile territory. Knowing this, his enemies would pretend to have forgotten him and allow him to advance; then they'd cut off his retreat and, in a panting silence, give furious chase. The boss bully was a mean guy whose mind, due to some hormonal slip-up, had escaped all moral structure. When you looked into his eyes, you could see the claws and fangs that hadn't found an outlet, and above all, you sensed a relentless vampire-hunger that made him a thousand years old. To him the playground was a patch of jungle teeming with birds at the mercy of his whims. He never let out a sound during class hours, emerging from his stupor only when the bell rang for recess. Then he came into his own. He was the one who tripped up Big Bellybutton and sent him sprawling, the one who pinched him savagely, snuck in vicious jabs, and streaked with cruelty what appeared to be just a few kids tearing around. There were two or three creeps of that stripe in the school, no more; each had gathered about himself an entourage of slightly less ferocious predators, a kind of pack eager to dominate and be dominated, and which obeyed him blindly. Each leader trailed his handsome sycophantic cluster like seaweed and seemed invincible on the playground; when recess was over, he camouflaged his haughtiness so as to pass unnoticed by the Teacher in the classroom. The boss bullies recognized their own kind intuitively and hardly ever challenged one another. Whenever that happened, there were memorable brawls after school that exposed our imaginations to the white heat of violence.

One day, Big Bellybutton — Lord have mercy on us — went off to recess with a bizarre look about him. Instead of hiding out near the Teachers, he ambled boldly across the playground and began to run-and-jump, to prance about the way the other carefree youngsters were doing. The little boy was simply amazed. He went off to join him, and they started to romp together. There was a strange twinkle in Big Bellybutton's bright eyes, and he often checked the bottom of one pocket. He was soon spotted. The boss bully went straight for him with the swinging gait of a desperado in a gun duel. The bully's henchmen joined him as he drew near. To their consternation, they saw that Big Bellybutton was putting on a show of indifference. The arrival of the meanies upset the guardian angel of the little boy, who was already in a sweat and tried to warn his poor buddy. But Big Bellybutton (who seemed blind, deaf, utterly oblivious) wound up corralled by the gang. He pretended to draw back, tried to scoot off, and then—grabbed, jostled—he produced from his pocket . . . a snake's head.

Chaleur!

The boss bully almost had a stroke. His ancestral ferocity was overwhelmed by the pure panic of a child. His lips flapped out a baby-squeak, and his suddenly rubberized legs began to wobble: he was done for. The Serpent's head was as big as *that*, all dried and wrinkly, twisted like you wouldn't believe. The jaws gaped open in a petrified gobble. Although the fangs were gone, you thought you saw them anyway. The attackers dropped like yellow mango windfalls. Some of them began the creepy-crawl of singed caterpillars. Others, sprawled on their backs, stared frozen with horror at the thing in Big Bellybutton's hand. He waggled it under their noses, brushed it against them, chased them with it. Carried away by his victory, he hadn't realized that the entire playground was now fleeing before him, that he was terrorizing friend and foe alike. *Chaleur!*

Alerted by the commotion, the Teachers hurried over, sticks at the ready, only to be stunned by what they saw undulating in the grip of that power-crazed hand. A few Teachers cursed in Latin; others, truly undone, fell back on their native Creole. The head of that tropical Bothrops did not so much frighten as appall them with its insane irruption into their learned world of apple trees, conifers, and garter snakes. Monsieur le Directeur himself appeared, overcoming his surprise long enough to whisper in a sepulchral voice, *Drop that ophidian this instant!*

Big Bellybutton let go of the head. As it fell, all present recoiled as one. Monsieur le Directeur grabbed Big Bellybutton by one handle and hustled him off to the office. Everyone else clustered around the frightful head. Then the Teachers shooed the children away, hushing their cries while looking back with round, incredulous eyes at the now stranded object. The school caretaker, who had scurried to his lodge, emerged shielded by a pail, which he clapped upside down over the head. With a sigh, quiet swept the courtyard on the instant. As though released from a spell, everyone looked around with the startled air of a sleeper awakening from a nightmare. The recess period seemed to come to an early end with the sudden ringing of the bell.

Class resumed despite the absence of Big Bellybutton. Without even giving the order to sit down, the Teacher started haranguing us about Negro-Creole customs and the hopeless perdition of that barbarous people. We hardly heard him, fascinated as we were by the solitary struggle of the caretaker out in the courtyard. He had covered his torso with a thick apron, pulled on big army boots and docker's gloves, and armed himself with a shovel. Half-squatting on the ground like a sumo wrestler, and leaning back to keep a safe distance, he had flipped over the bucket. Now he was pushing the head along toward the gutter out in the street with disgusted little swats of the shovel. His wife, shivering in the doorway of the lodge, watched him admiringly. Monsieur le Directeur interrupted this courageous maneuver, however, and, with equal parts precaution and audacity, popped this new trophy of his scholarly campaigns into a jar of formaldehyde.

Monsieur le Directeur's trophies: a chassepot, a slingshot, a tiny coffin, a *manicou* possum's tooth, a Great War grenade, a knife (Dog brand), a jar of red wasps, and an impossible number of marbles, comic books, photo-novels, yoyos, kites, plastic lanyards . . . *Répondeurs*, continue . . .

Early next morning, Big Bellybutton reappeared accompanied by his papa, who had been summoned to the scene of the crime. The father was the living image of the son (but gaunter), with his ways (but in a larger size) and his bearing (but more downtrodden). Dressed in Sunday best, holding his son with one hand and carrying a guano sack in the other, he waited with plantlike patience until the ritual trooping of the children off to class was over. His attitude was ceremonial, as though he were visiting a cathedral, and he looked around furtively, trying to keep his face impassive. Then we saw him ushered into the classroom by Monsieur le Directeur. Big Bellybutton trailed after them with bowed head. The Teacher bade us rise, then greeted Big Bellybutton's papa in overbearing French while his visitor stood there nodding. Undoing the big guano sack, the man produced seven cinnamon apples for Monsieur le Directeur and a *bocodji* yam for the Teacher, whose mouth watered with pleasure. Then, seized with a sudden burst of surely millennial rage, the papa laid hold of Big Bellybutton, extracted from his bag a switch of *ti-baume* wood, and inflicted upon the unfortunate child a thrashing that we were to talk about for absolute eons. The papa laid on with a will; you'd have thought he was trying to pull some damned weed up by the root. Let's say he was smack-and-whacking, slice-and-dicing, lash-and-bashing. Let's add that he was trouncing-bouncing, leathering-lathering, basting-pasting. Now and then he'd sneak a sidelong peek at the Teacher or Monsieur le Directeur to check on the sanctifying effect of this rawhiding, and sparked by the fire in their eyes, he'd thrash with fresh vigor. At long last, he stopped, for no particular reason. While Big Bellybutton stood motionless before him, the papa mopped his face, pouring out an inexhaustible warning in a solemn and almost incomprehensible Creole that echoed like a blasphemy within those Gallicized walls. After his papa left the classroom, escorted by Monsieur le Directeur, Big Bellybutton returned to his seat, hiccupping with stifled sobs. As their eyes met, the little boy saw that once again and doubtless for all time, the diminutive warrior remained undefeated in his heart of hearts.

Répondeurs:
Smackenwhackem!
Slicendicem!
Lashenbashem!

Big Bellybutton was the center of attention at recess. Instead of teasing him, the children stared goggle-eyed as though he were a traveling circus. They expected to see a spectral clutch of vipers tumble from his pockets, or a tangle of fetid *mabouya* lizards, or some spiky-haired tarantulas. He was now looked upon as the Master of Nasty Things from the Creole Wildwood, which distinction granted him a special immunity steeped in an aura of silence that was worse, to tell the truth, than any persecution.

Ever since the episode of the snake's head, the boss bully had watched his disquieting prestige wither away. It was said (behind his back) that he'd shat his pants right down to his shoes. Rumor had it that he'd been shaky-quaky for days-and-days, with the haunted eyes of a blackbird stuck out in the rain. Not a single youngster dared speak to him about it, but whenever he went by, the other bad guys held their noses and made a great show of checking his heels for telltale traces of his terror. Others would start wailing, pretending they were terrified by an imaginary snake. His gang seemed to have abandoned him to his disgrace. Alone, he loitered over by the water faucets or shut himself up in the toilets. Whenever he caught sight of Big Bellybutton, he returned to life, and we had the feeling he was ready to pounce bite pummel—but something always held him back, just as we now kept our distance from Big Bellybutton and the unpredictable contents of his pockets.

As days went by, the boss bully plucked up enough courage to take a surprise swing at Big Bellybutton, who didn't have time to duck. Logically, Big Bellybutton should have retreated to the protective cover of the Teachers' area to wait there until recess was over. Uh-uh! We actually saw him, tetanized with despair, hurl himself at his tormentor as though leaping into a suicide of flames. What happened next was a mix-up of thumps, gasping growls, and rolling around in the dust. All recess activity ceased instantly while kids gathered around to chant in unison the traditional cries of encouragement that had to accompany the blows: *iii salé iii salé iii salé iii sicré iii sicré!** The *iii* was supposed to start off rather low, increase in anxiety like the rumbling bellow of an ox, and explode into the titanic ovation of the *saaaléé!* Sometimes the *iii* was made to pant, to hesitate, to disappear, only to burst out with a trumpeted *siiicréé!* whenever a blow landed. Monsieur le Directeur outraced the Teachers to the battleground and danced around the combatants, looking for an opening. Suddenly he saw an arm shoot out, and he managed to grab that. Then he pinned down a flailing hand with his foot. Then he slipped his knee into a momentary gap between two heaving little chests. And then, backed up by the Teachers, he succeeded (with a loud sucking noise) in unsticking the brawlers, whom he dragged off as limp as dead fish. We could hear Monsieur le Directeur's whip cracking all the way up in his office.

There was a brief lull in the hostilities for a few recesses. The two enemies observed each other from afar. The boss bully

---

*It's salty, it's salty, it's salty, it's sweet, it's sweet! (Translation courtesy of the Omniscient One.)

stayed close to the courtyard walls, morose, secretive, touchy, sly, his eyes kindling at times with the fire of hot peppers. Big Bellybutton flung himself around with a serene indifference. The safety zone around him had grown larger. Only the little boy risked approaching him. The Teachers and Monsieur le Directeur kept watch on the two enemies from a distance with minatory looks. They were so attentive that the entire playground was affected: no one dared to run full tilt, to push-and-shove, let go and play flat out. High spirits were running low. Each child was on his best behavior under the multiplied eye of a vast conscience. This lull didn't last long, however. A rumor sprang up around the water faucets and spread by tittle and tattle: the curtailed conflict would be settled after classes one day. That's why the little boy, now an expert at chanting *iii salé iii sicré!*, began to linger outside the schoolyard gates.

... Monsieur le Directeur, I tell you he grabbed onto my kid's ear and tugged like he was pullin' yams, so over-much my kid's ear came halfway off yes, halfway off his ear is I tell you yes, halfway off yes, do you unnerstan such a t'ing?! he might of snapped his neck clean in two, popped his spine apart—now, that's my job yes (oh Lordy don't send me to jail!)—school's school they say and damn right, school's school, but a school ain't no butcher shop you hear me?—or p'raps it's a circus you runnin' here? a free-for-all? a bughouse? so I tell you plain, all due respect to your older years, I won't have such happen one bit more to him, not one smallest bit, because if he ever happen to step out of line again, it's me Bernadette, me yes a god-fearin' woman goin' to lay a hard hand on him yes, you see me here all sweetness but forgive me Lord I truly am a terror ...

The mamas picked their littlest ones up outside the school gates. The Big Kids went home on their own, taking along any younger children who were in their care. A few tykes whose mamas were late flung their satchels down at the foot of the wall and kicked up a ruckus on the sidewalk. Standing out in the crosswalk, the caretaker directed the traffic of rich folks' cars with the panache of a policeman. Monsieur le Directeur waited at the gate until the hubbub had died down, sent a last eye-sweep around the street, and returned to his office. The buzz was that he stayed there past midnight; some said he slept there, snoozing on a bed of red chalk sticks among the official registers, the globe, and the maps of France. The latest word had him sometimes spending Sunday in his office checking no one knew what and chewing on his worries as he prowled the deserted stairs. After school, the mamas would come up to him at the gate, braving that astringent and compelling eye. There they would offer him oranges, tangerines, small flowering plants, and consult him anxiously about their kiddies' future. There too, a mama furious with some Teacher would come, loudly demanding an explanation. This Teacher had pulled her son's ear right off his head. That Teacher had whapped so hard he'd raised a bump on the child like a budding horn. This other Teacher had disrespected her boy by calling him blacker-than-last-night or a natural-born idiot. And the indignant complainant would wave her arms around in front of Monsieur le Directeur, whose expression remained as unruffled as a glossy leaf of cabbage. She would explain that, since the days of slavery were long gone, no one had the right to touch a hair on her kid's head except the Goodlord, the Virgin Mary, Saint Michael (and that was pushing it!), plus her very own self. Monsieur le Directeur never said a word during these acrimonious barrages. He knew perfectly well that even the most outraged mamas revered the school. Not one of them ever threatened him with the scissors or bottle of acid customarily used in the settling of accounts. These women protested because it was in their nature to do so, a way like any other of drawing attention to their lives. Monsieur le Directeur never experienced the chill of a slicing blade, a taste of boiling water: momentary madness.

Most of the time, however, the children left school in a happy effervescence that trailed peacefully away in the fine foam of their departing footsteps. Then the late-afternoon silence would polish the mechanical movements of the caretaker as he latched the gate. When there was a fight brewing, though, things were different. And the most memorable of these blow-ups was the one between Big Bellybutton and the boss bully . . .

Luckily, Mam Ninotte was late that day. She must have had to straighten out some problem at the Social Security office or wait longer than usual for the evening whitefish to come in down by the banks of the canal. Loath to saddle himself with his youngest brother, Paul had slipped off toward home. The little boy was supposed to wait patiently in front of the school for Mam Ninotte. Even though he didn't like waiting, this delay was most opportune. News of the approaching battle had already reached him, so he kept his eye on the boss bully, who was keeping his on Big Bellybutton. If Big Bellybutton went left, right, or straight—there was the bad guy. As soon as Monsieur le Directeur had swept the street with one last glance and turned on his heel to go off to his lair, a panting knot tightened expectantly around the adversaries.

And the ritual of mortal combat began.

This ritual (I digress) had its apostles, its acolytes, its backtalkers, its goaders, its pushers-and-shovers, its poltroon-tipsters, its temporary griots, its counters-of-points-scored, its booboo-voyeurs, its official hangers-on, its scavengers, its way-out-of-control-madmen, its bloody-injury-advisers, its damage-assessors, its prognosticators, its mourners-without-hankies, its weepers-at-the-sight-of-blood, its utterly-useless-onlookers, and the ill-defined remainder of those for whom this language has no name.* This quasi-spontaneous brood hovered around the belligerents according to immutable and likewise savage Creole laws. These attendants charged the air, hardened hearts, raised conscience-clouding shadows from the murky depths. They made everything possible. They made everything inevitable. They were venomous.

One of the apostles fetched two rocks.

He placed the first at Big Bellybutton's feet, the second in front of the boss bully's feet.

"Here's your mama!" yelled the bad guy, pointing to the rock at his own feet.

"Here's your mama yourself!" replied Big Bellybutton, pointing to the rock he'd been given.

And the magical phenomenon took place.

*Allow me to be more specific: its *Apiyé-konchonni, Raché-koupé-fanne-dwèt, Mouch-bobo-senti, Dékalè-pa-anba, I-sinbôt-san-manman, Labous-ou-lavi, Fini-bat-san-batèm, Misérab-dyab, Koko-boloko, Sisi-menm-pri-isi, Sousè-lan-mô, Frisi-pété-doubout, Mandibèlè-salop, Afarel-gragé-rouj, Déchirè-dan-lapèn, Koupè-kou-bouloukou, Rachè-grenn-milé, Fourè-bwa-ba-makak, Dyèp-sal, Krapolad-la-fyèv, Grafiyad-tétanos, Pisa-vyé-fanm, Grokako-anmè, Piman-cho* . . . and all those regarding whose existence the High Cockalorum of Creole at the University of the Antilles–Guyana has not yet pronounced his verdict. (*Omniscient One's note.*) [Scum-supporters, Knuckle-gnawers, Smelly-sore-flies, Draggle-drawers, Mamaless-creeps, Your-money-or-your-life-bandits, Shameless-scenery-chewers, Miserable-fiends, Village-idiots, Wutless-good-fe-nuttens, Death-suckers, Grumble-guts, Lowdown-dutty-stinks, Bloody-scab-pickers, Racked-with-sobbers, Cut-throat-gloaters, Mule-ball-breakers, Backwoods-baboon-bumpkins, Nasty-wasps, Fever-toads, Lockjaw-scratchers, Pissy-old-ladies, Big-bad-naygahs, Hot-peppers . . . (Translator's note.)]

Big Bellybutton began to cast longing eyes at the stone sitting in front of the other boy's feet: it had become his own mama fallen defenseless into the power of his cur-dog adversary. Those longing eyes became gimlets of anxious vigilance, fixed upon their object. His body yearned after that stone, inhabited it. The same thing happened to the boss bully: that captive stone at Big Bellybutton's feet just racked his soul. His body puffed up with helpless rage. He kept staring at the rock. Watching it. Watching Big Bellybutton. Each one tried to dissuade the other from disrespecting the mama placed in his power. Each one tried to hold the other in check through his unwavering gaze. Each one tried to communicate to the other his determination to die for the stone that had become his mama. They might thus have neutralized each other, because any attack on one mama implied a smashing reprisal on the other. A perfect balance of misfortune.

The liturgical congregation would see to it, however, that the combatants didn't get stuck in a stand-off. *Let's go there! . . . Shake the lead out! . . . Get the stone! . . . Kick it! . . . Kill it! . . .* And this and that. They were pushed from behind, so that their feet would bump their opponent's mama-rock. They were egged on. Their grievances were expertly aired. Forces of darkness were invoked. Here the Creole language came into its own: the resentments that had built up beneath the French veneer had charged our native tongue with awesome hidden powers. Banished from the classroom, it could here (with rescuedwords, mutantwords, slitherywords, brokenwideopenwords, disorderlywords, ravinglunaticwords . . .) transmute good feelings into bitter chemical reactions, jolt a frightened sob into the growling of a mangy mongrel, flog a shiver into sheer epilepsy. Electrified, niggerlings became ravening wild animals, while the already not-so-nice guys turned even nastier. The suppression of Creole had revealed a virile efficiency in these illicit areas. We lapped it up like pigs at a trough. We rolled around in it like a mob sacking a forbidden temple. *Oh, here the language was a whole world!*

At the height of his towering rage, the boss bully gave a mighty kick to Big Bellybutton's mama-stone: *Whoosh!* Big Bellybutton let out a strangled cry: his mama had shot into the gutter. The onlookers shrieked with joy. Flap! Big Bellybutton booted the mama-stone at his feet, and the boss bully was treated to the spectacle of his symbolic mama sent hurtling God-knows-where. The adversaries were now fired up with a divine fury.

They leaped at each other, white-eyed and seeing red. Their circle of admirers began to chant the *Iiii saléééé*s, the *Wacka-wacka*s, the *Biwoua*s, the *Whap whap whap*s, the *Here's mine, this one's yours* that gloriously magnified the blows. The care-taker hove into view like a Horseman of the Apocalypse. He surged through the audience, plying his arms like galley oars. When he reached the incandescent energy of Big Bellybutton and the boss bully, however, he stopped dead, utterly stumped. In his bafflement, he tried a scolding in French, something about listening to reason. Hopping around the fray, he re-sorted to barking like a mad dog, then let out the shrill wheeeeeeeee of a fire-engine siren. Finally he exploded in the most unbelievable blast of Creole abuse we had absolutely ever heard. The mob was dumbfounded.

Big Bellybutton and the bad guy, still entangled, froze in fas-cination. The caretaker seemed possessed by a pack of zom-bies. This Creole eruption was accompanied by a hypnotizing vibration of his paunch. He was swelling with wrath, as though he'd popped out of one of those rigid carapaces that weigh so heavily on tired tortoises. After one last tremor, he recovered his composure, and taking advantage of the two adversaries' immobility, he easily plucked them apart. Sputtering curses, he forced them to march off in opposite directions. The crowd split up immediately: one group chased Big Bellybutton, laughing at his torn pants, while the other bunch made fun of the boss bully, who had a shiner bedeviling one puffy eye.

By the time Mam Ninotte arrived, it was all over. A quiet such as the little boy had never known now enveloped the school. He had stayed leaning back against the wall, not daring to run after the gangs of pursuing onlookers, and so had plenty of time to watch the school soak up the twilight. The sunshine was gone from the empty courtyard, the classrooms had been abandoned to echoes, the playground had grown vast in its solitude, and the big old building was now given over to an intimate life of shadows, roving creaking sounds, and the settling coolness of dusk. The caretaker had disappeared into his lodge, from which the aroma of frying codfish had begun to waft, embellishing the evening dew. It simply didn't seem like the same place.

The little boy had noticed that the mamas came to pick up only the smallest children, while the Middlings and Big Kids went home on their own in laughing groups, amusing themselves en route. That evening, he informed Mam Ninotte that he knew the way by heart and could come home alone like a brave little boy if need be. *You think so, h'm?* replied Mam Ninotte dreamily, because that proposition suited her just fine. And the next day, at eleven in the morning, he came home by himself for the first time, taking the same streets that Mam Ninotte used. He was afraid of getting lost and sped right along looking straight ahead, arriving at the apartment in no time. At five o'clock that afternoon it was the same story, and the next day, and the day after that. Reassured about the route (which remained the same, in fact, without going astray—as one might have expected—into those dark, wolf-infested forests Mam Salinière's tales had crammed into his skull), he began taking the time to look around him. Bustling feverishly before beginning its evening slumber, Downtown was alive with schoolchildren, women closing up their market stalls, ancient ladies and elderly gents coming home from an office or looking for a shop or pharmacy that might still be open. The *djobeurs*, the marketplace porters, sped off with their wheelbarrows to catch the last share-taxi blasting away on its horn in the middle of la Croix-Mission. Tailors received their rich mulatto clients, who tried on basted-together polyester garments in front of narrow, foxed mirrors in the piss-colored electric light. With priestly gestures, jewelers locked away precious sculptures, delicate, quivering brooches, incredible torsades; from their display windows they removed velvet trays on which lazed the splendors born of their creators' infinite patience. On balconies abloom with flowers, mulattas took the evening air, displaying a last taste of their slightly disdainful charm. Beside them, their old mamas cut short the flourish of a rose, disciplined the arc of a bougainvillea, pinched off bedraggled leaves. It was the moment (*Oh, I feel that tenderness!*) when the first aromas made their escape through the shutters: shin-of-veal soup, fried redfish, spicy pork fritters—Oh, I have all that . . .

Répondeurs:
Beflowered balconies
weep with desolate leaves . . .
Here's tenderness for you! . . .

Gradually, the little boy began to make detours: this street instead of that one; branching off for two streets before picking up the right one again; going straight ahead until the jetty came in sight, then cutting back on the track—all bold, intoxicating adventures, with the feeling of making oneself more grown-up on the sly and the tame fear of a benign unknown braved with a pounding heart. A secret's worth of pride bolstered his courage in the face of Mam Ninotte's questioning looks. *'Pears to me this lil' fellow's taken to wandering the streets . . .*

Taking a detour fleshes out Downtown. You discover a new Syrian, a street stall where Monsieur-Madame-China is piling up money. You discover houses without voices, their windows gaping onto a lifeless stillness. You discover tangled jackstraws of charred wood that bear witness to a recent fiery tragedy. You discover bars of light-streaked gloom where black men wearing small hats pulled low over their eyes sip quietly at peaceful intoxications. You discover, through the shutter slats, pensioners bewildered by immovable time. You discover shadowy dens where a cobbler sits buried by shoes. You discover that watchmaker who has become immortal beneath the remains of countless clocks. You discover the dockside warehouses that smell like tanneries, the stacks of barrels, the heaps of sacks, the gnarled strength of sweating niggers. You discover the melancholy return of fishing boats up the slack water of the canal when the catch has been too meager. You discover people with other customs, other colloquial expressions. Everything is similar to the little boy's own street, yet it's all different—not the same people but the same atmosphere, the same colors in other shades. Wooden facades are already being displaced by concrete and bricks. You learn about the other Downtown.

You make a detour in silence, withdrawn into yourself, on the alert inside yourself, attentive to yourself. Taking a detour is like examining one's conscience: in unfamiliar and more or less disquieting surroundings, one can rely only on oneself.

The little boy's detours did not really delay him much. The trouble started when he happened to wander into a den of iniquity: the nearby playground of the girls' school across the street from the police station. After classes, Middlings and Big Kids gathered in that courtyard to play marbles. The children tripped homeward, models of good behavior, under the watchful eye of Monsieur le Directeur, who had no idea they were only going around the corner to dig out unsuspected marbles from the bottoms of their satchels, trace in the dust lines and triangles of a precision that would have staggered the Teachers, wager the sheer marvels set out on the points of those triangles, and strive fiercely to win these prizes until twilight closed in. The yard had the ambiance of a fish market after a fresh catch of sea bream comes in. And that's putting it mildly.

Catching sight of Big Bellybutton amid this feeding frenzy, the little boy went over to him. Big Bellybutton was one of the crack shots. At a distance of more than a yard from a triangle, he zapped his targets, one after another. His shots (or his zigs, if you prefer) never got sidetracked into the grooves that spelled disaster. He held his shooter between thumb and forefinger, unsupported by his other hand, and snapped the marble off with a sweeping motion, casually, as though without even aiming, which provoked chagrined cries of *andièt sa!* from his opponents.* I should add that the stakes were suitably high.

Répondeurs: They also said, *Patat siwo! Prêl téléfon! I sinbot! Jésus-Marie-Joseph! Mi fè! La cho! Bay an socis! Laisse pleurer mon coeur! Bab sèpan!* . . . not counting moans and dramatic agonies. [Shit on a stick! Swee' stuff! Kinky-haired fink! Sombitch! Jesus-Mary-Joseph! Tough luck! Gettin' burned! Kill the dog! Cryin' time! Holy-moly! (Translator's note.)]

The most coveted marbles were the crystal-clear ones as pure as tears of affection. Their wager (was ever a thing so rare?) stoked the emotional fire of the competition. Let me tell you, a crystal was worth more than ten ordinary marbles. And to win such a gem, more than one player would have pawned his guardian angel, his First Communion cross, and probably his mama's love as well. A crystal was ethereal, reflecting the world back at you in virginal colors. Some of them had gobbled air bubbles that formed frozen sunbursts. A crystal was innocent, fragile, artless—and even the dumbest country bumpkin, the peskiest pain-in-the-ass, or the most heartless bastards would never have dared use one as a shooter. They were kept wrapped up in one's safest pocket, shown off only with infinite precaution, and anyone who wagered a crystal on a triangle point was convinced (vanity!) of his own invincibility. Whoever lost a crystal dragged his tail between his legs for three months, wallowing pitifully in personal misery. Which the Teachers, always well informed, would put down to the endless ravages of malnutrition.

Second best were the steelheads, ball bearings polished until they shone like black cat's-eyes. These were rarer than rare—you couldn't buy them. You had to cajole one out of a grease monkey by hanging around a garage or a distant factory. Depending on the strength and accuracy of a player's zig, a steelhead could smithereen another marble. These killers were of varying diameters, depending on what kind of ball bearing they'd come from. Their swap value was incalculable, because they made ace shooters and were thus avidly sought by the more thuggish players, the killers, the ruthless-rock-chewing-meanies, whose most refined pleasure was smashing their targets flat. Shooting with a steelhead wasn't easy: you needed a mighty forefinger and a Herculean thumb. Plus villainous cunning.

The large marbles we called *bôlôfs* possessed glorious hearts of miraculously swirling colors. Others were symphonies of greens, geysers of dense blues, fireworks of blood reds, and the little boy learned to cherish them all. Before joining the game himself, he observed Big Bellybutton's relaxed skill and the way he studied the entire triangular field of play. Big Bellybutton habitually knotted his marbles in a handkerchief that swung at his hip like a cowboy's six-shooter, and he pocketed his prizes lickety-split. The little boy soon understood why: anyone who had wagered and lost a treasure was always tempted to grab it, leave a *Sorry!* in its place, and take off. The captured marble had to be snatched up one-two-three before the disappointed loser even had time to think. Or to think twice.

About thirty Middlings and Big Kids clustered around five or six triangles in the playground. A special jargon flourished there, with its own codes, vices, and ceremonial expressions that I no longer remember. The crowd was made up of champions, masters, the rank and file, and the dregs (whose precious arsenal held nothing better than clay marbles—dull, sluggish things we called *kaniks*). This pecking order did not reflect the hierarchy of scholastic excellence established by the Teachers. A shining star at the blackboard might turn out to be a jerk at the triangle. A confirmed dunce, the utter despair of all the Teachers, might show true genius in his command of complex strategies. Big Bellybutton, for example, easily cut a swath through his opponents' forces, and without even seeming to take aim, he never missed.

Répondeurs:
Problem is,

I said *marble,*
But we really used *mab.*

As you approached the triangle, the enemy went right for you. If his mab touched yours, your stake was a goner (and so was your *joie de vivre*). So: the shortest path wasn't the safest, and the longest wasn't any better. You had to make allies of the stones, the gravel, the ant hills, the rat turds, the hard little seeds called Job's-tears, and the dust. You had to be able to take aim under the worst conditions. And never miss — not if you could possibly help it. A poor strategist might still meet with some success; a poor shot didn't have a chance.

First off: learn the rules by watching, without asking any questions; pretend you know the ropes, and bluff your way through. True mab knowledge must be soaked up through experience.

Then: dare to play, and act confident. Aim confidently. Walk confidently. Toss confidently. Knuckle down confidently. Woe to a wobbly zig, to a worried look, to any suggestion of hesitation.

Cultivate a detached attitude. Whoever makes a show of aiming — being ever so careful, with one eye closed in studious concentration — is setting himself up for resounding failure. Playing casually allows you to lose casually. Be cool.

Always: give the impression you're simply fooling around, testing your adversaries, just to see, before unleashing your prowess. In fact, your prowess grows with your luck, when your mab hits its target without your knowing how or why. Your path to the triangle becomes as easy as pie. You begin to pile up the other players' mabs, and these riches shore up your aplomb, which increases the quality, strength, and accuracy of your zigs. It's your luck, won over by your self-confidence. *Go for it!* The little boy—I can vouch for it—had some glorious moments.

Répondeurs:
Lose stony-faced.
Win stony-faced.
Cultivate the silence of a boulder
and keep your back bamboo-straight.
It chains up the hounds.

Sometimes the contest heated up, and the stakes were stiff: *bôlôf*, crystal, steelhead—or you're out of the game! *Roye*, it took guts to wager one of those three marvels. And balls to zig without a single tremor.

Répondeurs:
Believe in Lady Luck
she likes that
but don't ask her for anything.
Fascinate her.

There were always fools around to cock things up and make trouble, though. Sometimes it was a desperate soul who'd lost everything the day before, even his shooter mab. With this defeat still stuck in his craw, he'd come back itching to play some dirty trick. Then there was the sneak thief, who would cut a hole in his shoe sole, step on an outlying mab, and stroll off with his prey. There was the zig doctor, who'd nudge a mab into a tangle of roots with his foot when no one was looking and keep his mouth shut throughout the feverish search and supplications. A thousand mabs or shooters vanished like that from the humming playing field, thanks to the relentless enterprise of mabless tricksters skilled at filching, skilled at pocketing, skilled at making everything disappear into thinnest air.

Whenever a poacher pulled a fast one, it triggered misunderstandings, suspicions, heated words, promises of punch-ups, mama-insults, stifled sobs, doleful faces—a three-ring circus of despair. Injustice was on the prowl, luring players into hasty accusations. It felt good to hate. At the first smack, the battle was on. And on top of all that, there were tears.

Worst of all, though, was the *bawoufeur*, a kind of grabbalicious buccaneer. They would quietly insinuate themselves into the crowd, surround the choicest triangle, and pounce. Their code of honor required only that they shout *Bawouf!* before snatching up their spoils and scattering like a swarm of hornets, leaving their victims uncertain which marauder they ought best to pursue. The cry *Bawouf!* unleashed a wicked panic. Players threw themselves onto their mabs, hugging them tightly, tripping one another up in their protective frenzy. There was pushing. And trampling. And choking. Like drowning without water. Sometimes you grabbed the wrong mabs by mistake. If your bladder couldn't take it, you soaked yourself in shame. If your bowels gave way, you splattered yourself with dishonor. A few players, taking advantage of the confusion, gathered up mabs that weren't theirs. Others, finding their mabs already gone, took whatever they could get their hands on. All pursuit of the *bawoufeurs* was forgotten; there was always a marble still missing, a beloved crystal to search for, a problem of ownership to sort out. The *bawoufeurs* fell upon their booty with split-second precision. These adepts in the lightning strike were from the neighborhoods of Terres-Sainville, Bordecanal, or Trénelle and did not attend our school. They were ferocious bad guys, hard as nails. When we caught one of them, the fight was to the death. They were often older than we were, bigger and stronger. Their cataclysmic passage left behind total destruction: trampled grass, billowing dust clouds, ruined triangles, not a single marble on the ground. Here, a kid with tear-reddened eyes, mourning a lost crystal; there, someone anxiously checking what little he'd been able to save. The stillness of misfortune mummified the once lively crowd. Immobility; silence.

After a *bawouf*, it was hard to set up the triangles again. Play was suspended until the following afternoon. It was better that way, because strange to say, nobody had the heart to go on. A match continued after a *bawouf* always fell apart: the players were too nervous, too picky, too vigilant, and having recently experienced injustice first-hand, everyone felt vaccinated, entitled to respond to the slightest setback with more of the same, and in force.

Sometimes the cry of *Bawouf!* was a joke. Some fool would shout it just to see everyone jump like scalded cats. The ensuing uproar would peter out in a paradoxical combination of anger at having been afraid and the insane pleasure of discovering it was all a false alarm.

Between a *Bawouf!* and the wretched realization that you were ruined, there was often just a speck of a second.

> *Répondeurs*:
> A single tittle of time
> And you're torn to tatters.

Everything that childhood holds of joy, happiness, true exaltation, radiant pleasure, delight, euphoria, serenity, milky ecstasy, blessed peace, beatific innocence was, at one time or another, pounded to powder by the hatchet of a *bawouf*. Forgive me if I insist: despite the anesthesia of years gone by, it still affects me. Deeply.

We were preyed upon by one gang in particular. We never knew when they would strike. Big Bellybutton had finally figured out who their leader was: a kind of albino, with really reddish coloring. He lugged an enormous satchel around on his hip and seemed to be some big shot from the Lycée Schoelcher. This mangy dog ranged far afield to sow havoc. Big Bellybutton was the one who set the trap in which this *bawoufeur* and many another after him were taken. First off, ladies and gentlemen, to catch a *bawoufeur*, you must only pretend to play. Really playing means losing yourself in excitement and letting down your guard. Next, you have to load your triangle up something fierce, with crystals, *bôlôfs,* steelheads, prodigies of gala colors. You have to wait with more concentration than Nestlé's milk and an even greater purity of purpose. You have to let the vermin come up close, while you stay right on top of your marbles so you can sweep them up in no time. Lastly, you have to have placed a few rocks within reach as ammo for the big bombardment.

And here's the trap's split-second spring.

When their claws close on barren dust, the *bawoufeurs* are ignominiously stranded among us, a bit like albatrosses — those monarchs of the clouds who ride the tempest and laugh at arrows: exiled on the ground amid jeers, their thieving wings prevent them from . . .*

Actually, the albino never showed his face in the Perrinon playground again. And even today, when he walks by it with

* *Répondeurs*: Apologies to Baudelaire.

his children, you can bet he stares straight ahead with a vacant look in his eye—an eye dimmed by bitter memories.

Because the albino was taken in by that carefully set stage. He popped out from behind a tamarind tree. He sidled through the courtyard gates like a pale shadow. He melted into the throng with that characteristic expression of country-mouse innocence limned by La Fontaine. His minions arrived in turn, one by one, fanning out with angelic faces to await their leader's selection of the triangle to be pillaged. Big Bellybutton's was chosen, of course, for it was bursting with riches, like a tangerine tree aglow with December fruit. When the raiders screamed *Bawouf!* (leaping onto the triangle, which they trampled while we withdrew, all mabs safe and sound), their damnation was already being written in the book of fate. They found themselves inside a vicious circle: the whole courtyard was there, and Big Bellybutton was the leader. Then—I shouldn't say this—there was one glorious ball-breaking gut-busting ass-kicking lynching. There were electric shocks, napalm, slave trades, mini-genocides, deportations, ruinations, and complete routs. I shouldn't say this (we had a grand time . . .*).

Yes indeed, the albino forgot all about the Perrinon playground.

Répondeurs:
Me, for less than that
I would have forgotten it twice over . . .

Today I can explain this calmly: the word *bawouf* was a fundamental part of an unwritten law and, although reprehen-

Répondeurs: This isn't in the original.

sible, was not forbidden. You simply had the right to protect yourself from it. For example, it was dishonorable to scoop up mabs without shouting *Bawouf!* Whoever did so was a common thief subject to ostracism. Thanks to the ritual cry, a *bawouf* wasn't stealing but was more akin to a cyclone, an accident, or a run of bad luck. It was a misfortune built into the game, and it had the virtue of shaking things up, of evening out the playing field. A *bawouf* made as clean a sweep as a gullywasher in a drought, or—as the Poet puts it more sonorously—it was like the salubrious plow of the storm.*

Mabs meant coming home late after school. *Big trouble!* Around six o'clock, with darkness falling, the little boy would climb the stairs to his apartment with the already mournful look of cows in a slaughterhouse. He'd have to explain this delay to Mam Ninotte, who by that time was usually watching for his return from an upstairs window. She'd greet him at the door with her French-for-reproaches: *Monsieur, s'il vous plaît*; the funereally formal *vous*, and some *See here, my friend* stuff. Hands on her hips. The withering look of a childless woman. His cackling brothers would line up as though they were in a movie theater, in hopes of seeing a show. The first few times he wriggled out of a licking by inventing fibs: . . . *the Teacher had talked for the longest time about some business involving Gauls; . . . it had been really important to clean the blackboard; . . . an old* quimbois *witch had forced him to take a detour by trying to touch his head . . . and dis . . . and dat . . .* At first Mam Ninotte had pretended to swallow this guff. She'd tell him drily, *Don't let it happen again . . .* One day, however, he got all gummed up in a sticky fib and received his first spanking. After that, he stayed away from the accursed playground for three or four days. Just long enough to forget—and then it

*Aimé Césaire. (Translator's note.)

was back to the triangles, the ever more enchanting world of crystals, winning shots, and apocalyptic eruptions (with that glorious finale) of boldfaced *bawoufry*.

Fibbing to Mam Ninotte wasn't considered outright lying. All you had to do was give your imagination enough of a workout to excite her admiration. Seeing her little one putting his very own brain through its paces pleased her no end, and she never reproached him for a tall tale when he managed to bring it off. The bottom line: a story is a lie only if you tell it badly.

That's the tradition I follow.

Répondeurs:
I don't hang out with
liars
or mudslingers
or blabbermouths.
Between lying
and prickly okra hairs
I chose the prickles!

What made you cry when Mam Ninotte warmed your bottom wasn't the blows but the sudden breaking of a privileged tie. A hiding expelled the little boy from his mama's body. It was tough, my friends.

After-school games helped relieve his classroom misery. Nailed to his bench, with his mind constantly wandering, he looked forward to the end of the day the way we used to wait on long-ago Sundays for the Coco-Freeze man. In addition to recess, there was one other enjoyable period: milk time. Some bright light in the state children's welfare agency decided that the island's youngsters—stuffed with salt cod and green bananas, plantains, dasheen cooked with a little oil, and green mangoes—were suffering from malnutrition. This deficiency, in the experts' opinion, was the root cause of a cartload of learning problems, incorrigible drowsiness, and the Creole crust that encumbered our minds. Once behind his desk and subjected to the Franco-Universal beatitude of the Teacher, the little boy (well fed though he was on fish-vegetables-chicken-arrowroot and other delectable dishes prepared by Mam Ninotte) would go out like a cemetery candle: lackluster eye, droopy face, slumped shoulders. In fact, he and his fellow students did seem undernourished. The remedy was milk.

One afternoon the milk wagon showed up. We watched as large metal tanks were unloaded and the caretaker, supervised by Monsieur le Directeur, set up tables to serve as a counter. Each class was sent outside, one after the other. When the little boy's class took its turn, there was still complete puzzlement. You had to form a straight line, go up to the counter, receive an enormous tin mug full of very warm milk, and take your mug off into the courtyard to drink up every last drop in closely-monitored little sips. The children—feeling festive—didn't wait to be asked twice. So once a week, perhaps on Mondays, we received our lifesaving rations, and the afternoon was broken up by comings and goings that disturbed the whole school. The milk wasn't the thick, creamy liquid Mam Ninotte purchased from a woman from up in the hills but a lacteous chemical brew with a lingering aftertaste. On milk days, the Teacher had to abandon the regular class routine, so the little black boy had ample time to savor the milk with as much pleasure as if he were sucking civilization from the teat of progress. The Teachers waxed eloquent, moreover, on the subject of this all-purpose milk sent to us from France in the modern form of concentrated and powdered products from Nestlé.

France was a magic word. It sent things to heaven or hell. We had France-flour, France-onions, France-apples, France-whites . . . Whatever didn't have this carte blanche incorporated into its being was consigned to a native Gehenna. Nowadays we don't use that magic word anymore, nor do we allow it to entrench even the tiniest distinction in our minds.

In any case, leaving the classroom to drink some milk was still a treat, but perverse imaginations set to work to spoil everything. Live *anoli* lizards, it was said, were dumped into the milk as an unusual remedy for asthma. More than one wild-eyed witness claimed to have found in his mug rare furry caterpillars intended to improve the intelligence of sickly children. Others swore they'd seen the eggs of blotchy toads. The afternoon milk began to teem with Creole horrors: *molocoye* tortoise sweat, bamboo hairs like ground glass, crud from a he-mule's ears, feathers from black curlytailed chickens . . . The infinite profusion of maleficent materials used for sorcery by *quimboiseurs* was now suspected by the children of lurking in their diet supplement. *O speechless panic!* No one dared approach the Teachers about this. Although everyone pretended not to believe the rumors, the milk distribution—a real pleasure, at first—degenerated into a nightmare of distrust. The children inspected the liquid. They let it settle, calculating the chances of some loathsome object floating to the surface. They shook their mugs, whispering prayers and making occult gestures over them in secret. Despite these safeguards, they all found it difficult to raise the mugs to their lips. Just before swallowing, each child froze, terrified of feeling the thrashing flight of an *anoli* lizard across his tongue. And when their mugs were empty, the children felt vaguely depressed, liverish, with a living weight on their stomachs, as though they were possessed.

Problem: how to ditch the milk without being spotted. Aside from a few nitwits who would have swallowed even cobblestones, the students—holding their mugs at arm's length—began loitering around the water faucets, shutting themselves up in the toilets, leaning innocently over the gutters. Monsieur le Directeur and the Teachers (deep in discussion of the proceedings, with the heady feeling they were improving our lot) never realized that the culverts around the school were awash in the milk of our misery. And—cross my heart—out on the high seas, Caribbean pirate vessels must have trembled at the milky foam streaming from our shores.

Répondeurs:
I'd rather
break my ankle
on a breadfruit bone
than tell a single lie!

Our other distraction—and a welcome one before its worrisome purpose became clear—was the medical exam. We found ourselves out in the courtyard (barefoot, shirtless, unbuttoned pants ready to be dropped), lined up in front of a small shack transformed into an infirmary. There, a bored doctor checked us for scoliosis, myopia, caries, appendicitis and (*shit-on-teeny-tiny-tortoises!*) pulled down our pants to feel around for the silent ravages of some ball-gobbling hernia, or worse, a dick-strangling phimosis. Now, that put us on hot coals: *showing your willy!* Without even realizing it, the little boy clamped that part of himself between his legs. He who in his tenderest years had skibbled about butt-naked despite universal disapproval had gradually grown secretive about this natural embarrassment, which he now avoided showing to anyone. Only Mam Ninotte, when she snagged him for Sunday scrub-downs, still caught a fleeting glimpse of it. And there, in front of some unfamiliar doctor (or sometimes—even more awful—a lady doctor), you had to expose yourself. As the infirmary sucked in the line of waiting victims, the giggles of those up at the front died out, giving way to a spate of dry coughing. No brash, loud voices anymore. Showing your willy reduced everyone to the overwhelming fragility of childhood.

We used the word *Doctor*, which became *Doktè*, to designate supreme expertise. Among ourselves, we came up with quite an assortment: Doktè-mab, Doktè-punch, Doktè-snooze, Doktè-tricks, Doktè-talk, Doktè-zits, Doktè-bones, Doktè-sissy . . . and the dizzying paradox of the Doktè-dick.

The medical exam caused mortification in the line. You had to take off your shoes, which often liberated toes that reeked like a musty cellar—a sure invitation to teasing. A snooty child might be wearing humiliating baby panties beneath his trousers or, worse, underpants with flabby elastic prone to sudden collapse. Over here, a naked torso might reveal scads of pimples that meant irrevocable exile among the plague-stricken. Over there, another bare chest exhibited frightfully scrawny ribs, while still another displayed a laughably generous plumpness. Simply getting dressed again made you just *so* happy.

The shot was the hard part. *Oh! Ether!* There had long been rumors about this, but they'd been dismissed as silly old stories. Details, provided with an evil precision, still hadn't convinced us. Veterans of the ordeal had described it to the little boy in obituary terms . . . He has you come in. Busy fiddling with a big hypo. Doesn't even measure your height. Starts messing around with a humungous needle, wide as a crowbar, long as the trailing branch of a *filao* tree. Attaches his needle.

Sucks the poison up in it, gives you this fake smile, makes you turn around and stand up straight. You, you're starting to die. Your peepee's about to boil over. Your guts are cooking up diarrhea. Behind you, he's taking his own sweet time. Enjoying the way your shoulders're shaking. Says: relax your back, don't tense up. Waits some more to let you really suffer. *Oh! Ether! The perfume of this disaster* . . . Rubs you with it. It's chilly, not like ice, like a marble tombstone. That grabs you. You're already dead, so dead you wish you could die. Then suddenly, wham! Bang! Psssstt . . . Chuckling with delight, he jabs his needle into the juiciest bone in your back. And when he pushes down the plunger, you're a goner . . . *Oh! Ether! Fragrance of this misfortune* . . .

Waiting in line, we could hear stifled cries. We'd see really little guys come out of the infirmary, unable to hold back their tears. Others would burst out with hellishly red-rimmed eyes in potato-pale faces. Sometimes, we heard, the needle would stick right through and out your belly. Sometimes it broke off, quivering. Sometimes — when it got stuck in the bone — the lady doctor didn't know how to get it out, and so a whole bunch of students with needle-jamming bones had vanished into the infirmary oubliettes. Compared to this, even being in class looked good.

The whiffs of ether floated far and wide, searching tentacles, eager for living flesh. Who would have thought, then, that they would travel through time, preserving intact that ability to plunge the little boy into the anxiety of waiting on line outside an infirmary?

Répondeurs:
Oh, sing us the song of smells!

In recalling the smell of ether, you'll discover the emotion that will permeate your words. Ether is a dull feeling of worry and dread. For happiness, summon the aroma of hibiscus or of roasted coffee beans on Sunday afternoons. There's the odor of bleach, the smell of fresh paint that ushers in the New Year ... Camphor means sickness ... Do you remember the dreamy melancholy of vetiver? O bazaar of emotions, always precisely right, peacefully drafted for the empty spaces in the writing yet to be done.

Répondeurs:
Forgetting
sometimes
creates remembrance
it's emotion
exact
it's feeling
intact

Forgetting
sometimes
brings sweet sadness
it's memory
beyond memory

Forgetting
sometimes
vanishes into oblivion
it's the threshold of recollection
on the edge
of absence

Memory
you fashion yourself
with dabs
of oblivion

and
each one
strengthens what remains ...

The injection justified the use of strategic illnesses. Some boys returned to class staggering beneath the weight of a stiff shoulder. Some, half paralyzed, shut themselves off from the world like betrayed emperors. Some turned their desks into pillows, leaving the Teacher to his lessons. Some became allergic to school, moaning fetch-my-mama as they agonized on their tactical deathbeds. Some disappeared for almost a week, their mamas corroborating a distress that kept the absentees prostrate in bed. Vaccinations also legitimized related evasions. You wound up with an itchy shoulder, and you had to scratch. After a fever (parlayed into an epic production), big oozing booboos developed (you can still see the stigmata) that allowed the lucky one to come to school or stay home, to come and then leave again, in short—while the scar was healing under the scab—to avoid scholarly captivity. The little boy dragged out each shot, each vaccination, into endless syndromes.

"We don't say, *I'm talking for my body*; we say, *I'm talking to myself.*"

The Teacher hadn't given up his pursuit of Big Bellybutton, however. The latter had only just escaped death after a vaccination. His mama and papa had come to explain to Monsieur le Directeur that the vaccine had brought on a mysterious weakness that grew worse whenever school was mentioned. Monsieur le Directeur (preoccupied by the yams they had brought him and caring little for the uncertainties of medical science) advised the parents to keep the child home. Big Bellybutton's absence bothered the Teacher. He no longer knew whom to blast with his thunderous hymn to learning. His French lost some of its sheen. When Big Belly-button reappeared, the Teacher got back on track. Skipping over Big Bellybutton as usual during arithmetic, he hounded him when it was reading time.

The little boy loved to listen to the Teacher read them magical poems or selections from George Sand, Alphonse Daudet, Saint-Exupéry ... When he read, the Teacher sipped a fine liqueur. He took pleasure in savoring—letter by letter—the deployment of French in bucolic scenes. Devoted to the harmonious flow of syllables, he pronounced them clearly and emphatically, in accordance with some deeply felt rhythm. His voice paused dramatically at commas. For periods, it halted completely while his stern gaze swept over us. A semicolon produced a somersault of silence. His voice swelled as it approached an exclamation point—where it broke off abruptly. Parentheses sent him two steps to the left, where he spoke in an aside. Dialogues allowed him to assume a variety of accents, delivered through teeth like tweezers; bursting an invisible mold, he transformed himself like protean clay into a Provençal peasant, a solitary miller, a knight of the Round Table. When the paragraph was finished, he closed his eyes to contemplate with his mind's eye the solemn procession of what he had just read.

While he was reading to us, the Teacher himself would quickly become carried away; forgetting the world around him, he would embrace his text with an enthusiasm tempered by vigilance. Enthusiasm, because he abandoned himself to an author; vigilance, because a seasoned taskmaster remained on the alert, watching for sorry lapses in euphony or an idea undercut by weakness in the verb. Then an eyebrow would twitch with private disapproval. He took exception to some things in Hugo and Lamartine. La Fontaine and Chateaubriand, on the other hand, sent him into ecstasy. Actually, this pleasure of reading aloud was communicated to us quite unconsciously. What kept the little boy hanging on the Teacher's every word was not the text itself but the great gulps of pleasure the reader took in giving it voice.

Next! When we had to read, it was different. Identifying words, making liaisons, recognizing syllables, communing in the mystery of the silent *e*, doing breathing exercises with the aspirate *h*—all so many trials bound to end in disgrace because of our Creole accents. *Next!* The little boy's tip-of-the-tongue lisp increased his despair. His mumbling mouth softened up hard consonants while turning certain vowels to mush. Commas, periods, and suchlike slogged jerkily along while he struggled with the perplexities of sight-reading. His efforts were poisoned by mocking classroom commentary that the Teacher made little effort to suppress. *Next!* In fact, everyone made fun of everyone else: this one was done in by his Creole accent, that one by the quaver in his voice, another one stammered fit to choke, while so-and-so revealed an innate inaptitude for reading. *Next!* The fresh-from-France boys really shone in this department, however; they didn't understand any more than we did, and they mumbled just as much, but in the Teacher's opinion, their correct pronunciation, their peerless accents, the good taste they displayed in being unlike us, and the way they denied their own natures marked them as already imbued with the French universal essence of mankind. *Next!* . . .

We do not say, *to procure annoyances for oneself.* We say, *to get oneself into difficulties* . . .

Our reading material talked about farms, geese, harvest moons, wooden shoes, hares, chimneypieces, squirrels . . . The fresh-from-France kids tried to look as though they understood, but the other youngsters discovered these enigmas in deeply baffled delight. Our laborious sight-reading left us all at leisure to grab at the dreams flitting through our classroom. Lured by the sound effects of these magical readings, fantasies, visions, and chimeras began to nest among us. They brought with them other seas and shores and a taste for living prey. They delivered auguries. They untangled portents. They snatched at us with their beaks and claws. And we, sitting perfectly, drunkenly still — we devoured them. Once his turn to read had come and gone, the little boy flew away like many another into this nebulous world, from which he brought back only a vacant stare. *Next!* Quite a few were startled to find it was their turn. The Teacher had to pluck them down from way up high. They tumbled from their dreams to land — splat! — on their open books, haggard, unable to find the correct place.

The Teacher hunted down dreams. He could feel them passing by. He sensed them hovering over our heads. He divined their silent presence in the drawers, the inkwells, beneath the desks. He suspected who was possessed by them, who was slipping slowly away to them, who had drowned himself in them. That was when he called on you. The dreams took flight.

Often, he changed the reading order for the sole pleasure of catching a dreamer.

Répondeurs:
Ho, shooting down a dreamer . . .
Such fun . . .

Sometimes the teacher tried to compare the reading material to our reality. And that's how he came to question Big Belly-button.

"So, we've seen that on winter evenings on the farm, Petit-Pierre enjoys slipping between the cozy sheets of his nice, soft bed. Are things the same for you, my friend? Do you remember an occasion when your bed became a pleasant nest for you?"

He asked Big Bellybutton to follow Petit-Pierre's example and describe his house, the place where he did his homework, the light in his room, how he got to school. There were bursts of hilarity as Big Bellybutton, prodded by the astonished Teacher, unveiled the nitty-gritty of his life. His bed (he called it a *kabanne*) was a pallet of dried grass that he spread out every evening on the floor of a one-room shack, next to the pallets of his ten brothers and sisters. His parents slept on some kind of bed with feet, behind a curtain of oilcloth. In the morning, the pallets were rolled up and put in a corner or placed outside to air after a bedwetting. No sheets, because the heat was oppressive; sometimes, when the evening damp grew dangerously chilly in December, he would cover himself with a square of madras. In the evening, the children would all jostle sullenly for space in which to do their homework around the feeble glow of a single kerosene lamp that filled the shack with smoke. In the morning, Big Bellybutton had to fetch endless pails of water, tether an ox to graze on a patch of grass, pick fresh rabbit fodder, water some goats, and then dash a few kilometers to school. To do these chores, he had to get up before cockcrow and even before the early rising pippiree bird.

We laughed our heads off.

Cracked up.

Howled.

The Teacher, well, he was appalled. His world of idyllic farms, windmills, shepherds, charming autumnal scenes beside peaceful ponds—came crashing down on the spot. The age-old barbarity of the cane fields ... the poverty of the shacks ... the dark night of Creole niggerdom: it all seemed to have traveled through time to come crowding around the gates of Downtown. From that day on, the Teacher gave up trying to explain the reading material to us, remaining instead aloof on the empyrean heights of the wonders described therein. We saw that he was more indulgent toward Big Bellybutton about his absences, his drowsiness, his thick-headedness. The Teacher felt he was acting compassionately in abandoning the boy to his fate. He no longer called on him or questioned him but consigned him to the oblivion of which the rest of us all dreamed.

To Big Bellybutton, the Petit-Pierre we read about seemed like an alien from outer space, but as we read farther along in these sacred texts, it was Petit-Pierre who began to seem normal to Big Bellybutton and most of his classmates. Where are my *Répondeurs*?

Think about that first book. The heavy type, each letter standing out. The illustrations on every page, filling our heads with a world so far from our own. Its forests. Its animals. Its seasons. Its hierarchies of colors that assigned the shades of our skin to ugliness, and danger, and evil. *Ah me, what bewilderment!* All agog, the little boy had plunged more than once into each one of these illustrations. He had worn wooden shoes, scythed hay, gathered firewood, sheaved wheat, labored in vineyards, trampled vats of grapes. In vast, desolate tracts of wintry forest, he had celebrated the unchanging greenery of a handsome fir tree. Amid sweeps of virgin snow, he had sculpted snowmen with icy hearts. He had picked violets and inhaled the scent of rosemary in the spring. He had, in the rosy-cheeked, blue-eyed days of a blond childhood, gamboled through fields of May flowers. To welcome the New Year, he had sung, *Happy New Year to all the roses that nestle at winter's breast* . . . Often, down at the island's shores, he'd thought he could see France, so-close, really-so-close, oh-really-really-close, in the blue shadow clouding the horizon.

His head filled up with the world in those pictures. His mind — skilled in wandering, adept at spinning gold from the slightest straw of reality, a powerhouse of dreams — began to roam this universe that was becoming his true life. He drew in it. Dreamed in it. Thought in it. As for his body, that was drifting around in his frayed, shoddy, useless Creole world. His body had faded into the background (as stranded as a sand bank at low tide) in a reality that no longer excited his mind.

His slate became a companion of good times and bad. The Teacher would set the class a problem, and everyone would put chalk to slate in a mad dash for the solution, sneaking the occasional peek at his neighbor's progress. You sat hunched over your slate. You wrapped your arm around it and shielded it with your body, as much to protect a correct answer as to hide a possibly foolish one. Then, the wait: hearts pounding at the thought of success — and pounding as well at the more likely prospect of failure. At the Teacher's signal, there was a prompt and clattering response, ending abruptly in tense silence. And the Teacher would begin his dreaded tour of the forest of slates held aloft. He examined each one. Bestowed his commendations. Ridiculed mistakes. Passed judgment.

Ah, the satisfaction of the right answer. The sweetness of a faultless slate. The Teacher never made a show of praise, saying simply, *Well done, my friend.* And that was enough. You were content. Sometimes the little boy was eaten up with longing for the right answer. He would give it his all, driving himself, eagerly anticipating his *Well done, my friend.* And sometimes he repressed this desire to succeed: carried away by bad thoughts, he'd withdraw mulishly into himself and cling to his obscure rage with brutish determination. The incorrect slate became his flag of rebellion.

And then there was the empty slate, which sprang from a stymied brain, a sluggish bit of chalk. You emerged from an absence, as bereft as a *manicou* possum when the custard apples aren't yet ripe. The order to hold up your slate came too soon. In a conditioned reflex, you hoisted an empty slate over your own annihilation. That slate was the heaviest of all.

A blank slate put some zest into the Teacher. *Mathematical confirmation: from nothing can only come nothing. You beggar, your mind is as empty as your slate.* Sometimes he stood there pretending to read carefully, nodding his head as though in admiration, and then sweetly dealt the death-blow before a silent audience: *Would you be so kind, you vandal, as to repeat out loud for me the answer you have put forward for our consideration?*

The Teacher had a short memory. A *Well done, my friend* bestowed no blessing of lasting effect. One might fall from grace with the very next slate. *Will you look at this simpleton's answer!* Or, *What has this dolt come up with now?* Or else, *Oh, citizen — do you ever listen upon occasion to what I say?* Or worse, *Whoa, there must be some mistake here: this is not a braying contest in the perfect ass championship . . .*

We went to school to shed bad manners: rowdy manners, nigger manners, Creole manners — all the same thing.

From time to time, the Teacher would exclaim the words of Jules Monnerot: *France always, France in all ways!* O land of Vercingetorix, Joan of Arc, Clemenceau, ancient center of Latin civilization from which sprang Malherbe, Racine, Hugo. O great friend of progress, proud homeland of Pascal, Berthelot, Pasteur, wellspring of the arts, peerless arbiter of taste, sweet land of the liberties of 1789, cradle of the great and noble Schoelcher! . . . The Teacher was declaiming to himself.

The vibrant spirit of learning and our Creole beings seemed to be in insurmountable contradiction. The Teacher had not only us to contend with but also the entire country. He saw himself as embarked upon a mission of civilization, something like those missionaries who bury themselves in savage lands. Day after day, from one watering hole to another, without an ounce of pleasure, these finders of lost souls pressed on. The effort demanded was colossal, beyond mere brute strength. Since he had to slog through the mire every second he spent among us, each of his words, gestures, commands, and murmurs was armored with the Universal. The Universal was a buckler, a disinfectant, a religion, a hope, an act of supreme poetry. The Universal created order.

In those days, the blue-eyed Gaul with hair as yellow as wheat was everyone's ancestor. In those days, Europeans were the founders of History. The world, once shrouded in darkness, began with them. Our islands had been veiled in a fog of nonexistence, crossed by phantom Caribs or Arawaks themselves lost in the obscurity of a cannibal nonhistory. And then, when the colonists arrived, there was light. Civilization. History. The humanization of the teeming Earth. They shouldered the heavy burden of this world they were raising to the lofty heights of consciousness. We had to strive stoutly so as not to abandon them to the solitude of this responsibility. The Teacher wanted to carry the world on his shoulders, too.

Christopher Columbus had discovered America, drawing into the world millions of savages—in darkness since time immemorial, excluded from humanity—who had been waiting just for him.

"Do you know, you Ostrogoths, that they brought to the New World iron, the wheel, the ox, the hog, the horse, wheat, rye, indigo, sugar cane?"

"The superior races—this must be said openly, following the example of Jules Ferry—have, with regard to the primitive races, the right and the duty of ci-vi-li-za-tion!"

The little boy loved to hear the Teacher tell them the History of the World. Everything seemed simple and just. Everything tended toward ineluctable progress. His flights of fancy were then stilled, and he listened to this fabulous story that formed the basis of the Teacher's instruction. Often, this song of History spilled the little boy right into the action of his movie-going hours: the American Indians of Buffalo Bill, the Zulus of Tarzan, the Chinese of Marco Polo, the Moors ambushing noble knights . . . These savages demonstrated bloodthirsty brutality. They represented darkness confronted by the light. Howling madness struggling against the progress of civilization.

Répondeurs:
The Universal created order!

The desk was made of a soft wood, blackened by age and easily carved. Into it you could cut your name, words, drawings, the geometry of some ineffable emotion. With the point of a compass. With the tip of a pin. With the end of a broken pen nib. The desk was a skin tattooed by the reveries, the daydreams, the mute amazements that charged our hands with the burrowing energy of dazed engravers.

Répondeurs:
The Universal created order!

This difficult task of civilization sapped the Teacher's strength without our noticing it. One time we saw him cough. Another time he had lost his voice because of some throat ailment or other. Then he disappeared for two days. *La chaux!* It was Monsieur le Directeur in person who came to teach our class. Monsieur the Directeur was the Teacher times ten. Meaner, stricter, more at ease with our muteness. He would go to the blackboard and lecture us, seeing in our spectral silence a perfect occasion for the imparting of Knowledge. He was shocked to find how little we had learned since the beginning of the school year. *You haven't heard of this? You aren't familiar with that? My word* . . . He welcomed the Teacher back after his illness with a long conversation in the upstairs office, thus giving us half a morning's vacation. Thus inflicting upon us as well—in a backlash invigorated by the Teacher's return to health—a redoubling of his ferocity.

Knowing that the Teacher had been sick now allowed us to see him as susceptible to the ills of humanity. Until then, we had viewed him as indestructible, perched immaterially on the summit of Knowledge. The question of his vulnerability was raised throughout the playground: each of us asked himself this question, and each of us answered it. It was decided, unanimously, to kill the Teacher. (Ah, children don't mess around, no indeed!)

Répondeurs:
Step on a crack!
Break his back!

Big Bellybutton, that past master of Creole magic, told us the secret: *We had to get a hold on him.* This meant tying up a person's vital energy, rendering him helpless before an onslaught of ailments. When someone was tied up, any passing misfortune would pounce on him. Like a lonely attack of elephantiasis looking for company. On him!

Répondeurs:
A bone-shattering fall?
On him.
Swollen balls?
On him.
A pneumony?
On him.
A running sore?
On him.
A pleurisy?
On him.
An achey head? A chigger? A spell of fever?
On him! On him! On him!

In a flash, the person would wind up more dilacerated than a banana leaf in a hurricane. The secret of tying-up had been vouchsafed to us by Big Bellybutton after a torturous ritual. At recess, we all had to leave class right foot first; anyone stepping into the courtyard with his left foot was eliminated. Then we had to find a spot where the spoken word would not drift up or down or into eavesdropping ears. Big Bellybutton leaned his back against the wall in a corner of the toilets and began his initiation with a sign-of-the-cross so speedy it was incomprehensible. Then we had to do the same. The Revelation was delivered in a whispery, toneless voice spiked with a few grunts reminiscent of garbled church Latin. Big Bellybutton's popping eyes gazed into the ancient past. With crossed hands, he gripped the arms of each of us in turn with unbearable strength. What we had learned now began to weigh on our thoughts, leaving us silent and prematurely aged, while Big Bellybutton, restored to his childhood, went skipping off.

The little boy had resolved never to reveal so sinister a secret. This intransmissible knowledge made him conceited: a heavy step, downcast eyes, a hollow voice, solemn gestures. Mam Ninotte, ill-informed about the side effects of this arcanum, decided he was suffering from worms and dosed him with wicked purges: evil-smelling tansy syrup mixed with infamous castor oil. Wedged into his chamber pot, the initiate managed to conserve only a scrap of dignity.

To tie up a Teacher (you're not hearing this from me), you had to cross your fingers and hold them like that, thrust deep in your pockets; stand on your left foot in front of the school; murmur over and over again before he appeared: *Three dogs three cats tie up the Teacher . . . Three dogs three cats tie up the Teacher . . . Three dogs three cats tie up the Teacher . . .* (You didn't hear this from me . . .)

This whisper had to be like an order given to the world, delivered with all possible conviction and radiating outward like a blast of heat. In those days, life could be affected by the power of words.

Répondeurs:
I admit
I am still in thrall to

the most ancient memory
and the perfect cipher

Two or three of us would be there each morning, tying up the
Teacher. The effects of such an assault were not easily quan-
tifiable. Weeks might go by without our victim suffering any
attacks. None of his hair fell out. There was still a spring in
his step. His hands never faltered. The spells we so carefully
cast on him seemed ineffective. And then every once in a
while, just like that, one day when we least expected it, he
wouldn't appear.

Teacher's absent!
Mèt-la pa la!
Gone and disappeared! . . . Answer me . . .

Oh, the thrill of lining up before an absent Teacher! Our
line was perfectly silent, impeccably straight. Other classes
looked on enviously. Oh, how wonderful to take your seat in
a decapitated class! The reasons behind the Teacher's absence
were never very clear. Rumors mentioned the funeral of an
elderly uncle, pedagogical conferences, or bouts of grippe that
obliged him to miss a day or two, a week at most. We were
the only ones who knew the truth behind these absences. And
in our triumph we turned upon the rest of the school the
venerable, hooded gaze of magicians and *quimboiseurs*.

When the Teacher had been laid low, our magic attacked his
replacement: Monsieur le Directeur. Alas . . . that one was
forever invulnerable. Not a single chill. Not the slightest snif-
fle. Big Bellybutton's diagnosis: he must have been born with
a caul, and such a birth was proof against us all. Oh weep, my
heart . . .

Répondeurs:
Respect!
Some people have found their niche in life . . .

The little boy was quite a conscientious spell-caster. He became the commander of chance, the master of misfortune, the guardian of good luck. He directed his destiny the way one leads around a mule. He was the captain of fate. He spent oodles of time giving orders to trees, marbles, triangles, candies, numbers, and the Teacher's brainteasers. He tried to destroy the predators who dominated the playground. He attempted, throughout entire seasons, to conjure away the rain—or to conjure it up. To charm butterflies, tame hummingbirds, make himself invisible to the craftiest rats. He desired ardently to float through the air, glide over the *mornes* with the adventurous trade winds, and walk through walls. He did his utmost to stop time (so useful for loitering after school). And he was able to make the days pass more quickly. No one ever realized this, of course, because the world went on its merry way unchanged.

He tried to find a way to stay at home while he was in school. Or vice versa.

"We don't say, *He was stuck in a tar patch* . . . We say, *He was in a difficult situation.*"

The Teacher was not unacquainted with the world of Wonders. He told us of druids, fairies (Vivien Morgan le Fay Alcina Melusina Urgèle Urgande Holda . . .), pumpkin-coaches, and an enchanter called Merlin. He frightened us with the wicked fairy Carabosse, will-o'-the-wisps, gnomes, hobgoblins, elves, werewolves. He tantalized us with the power of magic wands and fed our hypnotized innocence on stories of witches' sabbaths, black magic, and mandragora. He described how broomsticks zoomed through the air beneath the rumps of crones. As for Big Bellybutton, out by the water faucets he would rumble on in forbidden Creole about zombies, three-leg-horses, the dangerous water sprite called a *Manman Dlo*, flying sorceresses, *soucougnans*, stoppin'-coffins, clairvoyants, black-hands, never-healing-wounds, spell-books, bedeviled-dogs. He told us up-country tales of the elegant Glanglan Bird, the occult virtues of curlytailed chicken feathers, the foolishness of Brer Tiger, the trickery of Brer Rabbit, the brainstorms of those rascals Ti-Jean-Lorizon and Ti-Sapotille. Oh, I was enraptured by his riffs on the Woods-master, the *chenille-trè-fle*, the avenger Makandal, the monstrous *Bête-à-Man-Ibè*, the incubus called a *dorlis*, the Antichris'. He prayed to Saint-Dominique's-cuckoo and Saint-Conch's-shell. He sighed over the lamp-charm that when dissolved in wine and holy water could make any female reticence submit to male authority. Big Bellybutton's marvels — *hair-raising, jaw-dropping, oh my yes!* — worked their way into our vitals and taught us to be wary of the world, while the Teacher's flamboyant wonderland dazzled our minds, whirling us far and away in a boundless, high-seas intoxication.

To the little boy, the Teacher's books were like fountains of life, while the Word of Big Bellybutton seemed often to take on — oh, often! — the aura of legend.

To you, dear Teacher, I owe my loving regard for books. Thanks to your reverence for them, they will always be alive for me. You handled them delicately. You opened them with respect. You closed each one as though it were a book of prayer. You put them away with a jeweler's care. At day's end, you carried them off like treasures sacred to a timeless ritual of which you were the last hierophant.

I'm grateful to you, Big Bellybutton, for your underground language. You fled through it, took refuge in it, resisted with it, inhabited it with infinite familiarity, and this fierce deep-rootedness endowed your language with a latent strength whose combustive power I would realize only many years later, when your face and the sound of your voice were already forgotten. (You were not a storyteller — you were a repository of memories.)

"Grreat heavens, you dunderheads, we don't say, *Woulo!* We say, *Brravo!* Isn't that much better?!"

One day of high conjury (the little boy had backed up his spells with the mediumistic support of a tamarind tree), the Teacher was stricken with lumbago, so a substitute took over the class. This fellow was a bit strange. He dressed quite youthfully, preferring baggy shirts to a suit and tie. He sported a rebellious goatee and bottle-bottom glasses over toadish eyes. He taught us for little more than a week, and what he taught us shook our world. Without using Creole himself, he tolerated ours to help us understand French. He had read a poet named Césaire, whom he quoted constantly, and he talked about something called *Négritude*. Occasionally he showed up wearing African boubous. He did not speak disdainfully of Africa or the rest of the world. During our reading period, he would change Petit-Pierre's universe at will: mulberries became calabashes, while apples and pears turned into dates. The images he read out loud were different. *Knee-high to a grasshopper* became *knee-high to a sugar-cane beetle; thin as a wolf in winter* became *thin as a desert hyena*. He claimed that our ancestors weren't Gauls but people from Africa. He contradicted the Teacher with vigor, persistence, and a fierce joy. But he never tackled either the Universal or its world order. We never understood what it was he wanted of us. As he was certainly not born with a caul, the home-grown Teacher was transformed into a comet: ephemeral and about as useless.

Wherever the home-grown Teacher saw *White*, he put *Black*. He championed the broad nose over the beaky variety, nappy hair over the silky kind, and emotion over reason. In the face of Europe, he set up Africa. In order to live with the French language, he resorted to a subversive variety he described as "revolutionized." He belonged to the opposition. Yet we never felt we were dealing with anyone other than the Teacher. It was as if the afternoon shadow of our martinet had risen from the ground, coming to life like an angry ziggedy-devil released from its bottle. He cramped us in the same way. Conformed us in the same way. The magicians condemned him out of hand.

> *Répondeurs*:
> Out of nowhere:
> the scent of a tangerine
> brings the joy of Christmas,
> such a wonderful promise.

Time-to-time, the home-grown Teacher would give in to our massed silence. *All right, if you really must, say it in Creole!* But we'd still sit there tongue-tied. The permission to speak Creole suddenly made us feel ashamed, like a confirmation of our hopeless failure, a willingness to be kicked aside into the gutter.

> *Répondeurs*:
> What
> had Creole become
> deep down inside us,
> crushed?

The little boy had become a walking secret. He kept quiet, hiding the thoughts gusting around in his head. Although Mam Ninotte asked him about school, he told her nothing, as though not wanting to sadden her. He felt he was betraying the unspoken mission she had given him: to succeed in school. She had never said to him, *You must make it, you must succeed!*—but she went to such pains to get him ready, took such care to accompany him, looked at the Teachers with such devotion, that the little boy could tell the stakes were desperately high. Losing hope that he would confide in her, Mam Ninotte tried to read his eyes, his inky fingers, and above all, his clothes. To the little boy, clothes did not exist. In other words, they didn't keep him from living.

He rolled in every patch of dirt. He clambered up every wall. He skidded down every slope on his bottom. Mam Ninotte had to wage all-out war to keep his shorts from falling apart. As for shoes, she was quickly forced to rely on clunky and almost indestructible footwear that her son used less for walking than for kicking the whole world, and especially mama-rocks.

Putting on those gunboats was like slipping into armor. An ankle encased in that stiff leather became invincible. A silent battle then broke out between the little boy and the shoes. He tested them severely, as much to quell their resistance as to explore the powers of a foot protected from pain. He banged them up, stomped them into puddles, scraped them on gravel. The clodhoppers fought back by bruising a toe joint or planting stinging blisters on his heels. Then they began to brew up terrible heat rashes that came to light in the evening, when he took off his shoes and liberated a smell—*Good-God-Almighty!*—that put the entire household in a funk. *That child will kill us all!*

It was way-beyond-hot, but sandals were frowned upon. A sockless foot was a disgrace, and a sleeveless shirt was just not in good taste. The climate was willfully ignored. And things haven't changed a bit.

The shoes started out a handsome tan, with shiny metal rings around the lace holes. As the battle wore on, the light brown leather grew dull, muddy, then sort of cowpat colored. Soon, like the other pupils, the little boy was clomping around in what looked like two hugely swollen yams. But clodhoppers never died. They just got a little too small and wound up stuffed under the bed in the well-deserved retirement of combat-weary veterans.

Subdued while in school, the little boy opened up like an umbrella outdoors, in the street, at home. Everything outside the school became an even bigger school. What counted was his busy inner life: things that interested him, things he cared about, things the Teachers never knew were there.

He was bundled into reading and writing when he knew nothing about himself, or life, or grownups, or the world they were bringing to him.

"Let's do things properly: don't speak to me of *titiris* anymore; use the word *alevins*. Someone lacking in self-respect is not *disrespecting himself*. And if someone vexes you, say that he is *irritating*—not, dear God, that he is *pestersome!* O savages!"

The Teacher never congratulated Mam Ninotte. He was simply polite to her. When considering the little boy's aptitudes, he did not swoon with delight the way he did with the two or three class geniuses. So Mam Ninotte diligently cooked up for her young dunce some most delicious lamb's brains intended to boost the powers of his own. As brain followed brain, it seemed to the little boy that he was getting a tad smarter.

When he questioned Mam Ninotte anxiously on this point, she agreed that she could see his intelligence growing by the minute, like a weed. Only the Teacher, blind as usual, never remarked upon it.

In spite of Mam Ninotte's culinary skill, it took courage to swallow that weekly serving of slimy brain salad. Particularly since Jojo the Math Whiz had explained to him that an ovine brain would confer upon its consumer only the bleating virtues of a sheep. Paul the Musician hadn't denied this. The Papa, consulted on the question, declared himself unfamiliar with Mam Ninotte's magical thinking and asked to be excused from the debate. The little boy thus kept one eye on the disputed progress of his intelligence and the other on the modulations of his voice. When he awoke, he would whisper hello to himself to make sure it didn't come out in Sheepish. Just on the off chance, he also checked his ears and the texture of his hair.

On after-brains days, the little boy felt peppy. More on top of things. He dared to look right at the Teacher and wait for a question. There was a gleam in his eye and some starch in his backbone. The Teacher, who no longer expected anything from him, never learned how to use these moments of intelligent grace. When the effects of the brains wore off, the child had to retreat once more into survival mode, blend in with the wall, become desk colored, half invisible, more discreet than a caterpillar tucked beneath a tender leaf, losing hope of ever becoming a butterfly.

"Ye gods! The correct word is *pulp*—not *goop*!"

But the brains weren't all. Cod-liver oil was the best of tonics— and the worst of trials. On those days, Mam Ninotte didn't even negotiate. Silent, determined, she gave no quarter. You were grabbed by one wing, clamped between two knees. The Baroness sometimes gave assistance to the law in its murderous operation. Held fast, your nose pinched shut, you couldn't help swallowing that gummy horror. It slithered inside you like cold despair and spread mortuary smells all through your body. You no longer knew what to do with your mouth or the flavor of your tongue. You stood there all agape, afraid of swallowing again and reviving that taste. Then Mam Ninotte would give you a sweet over which you would agonize queasily for an hour or two.

Sometimes the little boy wriggled too much, causing part of the spoonful to dribble down his chin. And his neck. *Fer!* Now his head reeked of cod-liver oil. Then Mam Ninotte would capture him for a second dose, which meant he'd get a spoonful and a half. So he learned to stop struggling, go into a trance, and let the stuff slide down his dead throat. He came back to frenetic life only when he received his candy.

Répondeurs:
Fer!

The class had quickly settled into ranks: the smarties, the numbskulls, and the hopeless duds. More or less consciously, the Teacher no longer paid attention to any but those from whom he expected something. The rest were abandoned to Creole fecklessness. He questioned them infrequently, no longer seemed to care when they didn't understand something, and took little notice of their occasional correct replies. If a numbskull or a dud chanced to produce the right answer, he was criticized for his accent, his manners, the way he'd raised his hand, his slouching posture . . . and a sarcastic barb from the Teacher would emphasize the rarity of the occasion.

A smarty floundering in a wrong answer was nevertheless congratulated for his participation, his zeal, and the spark of light he brought to the general dimness. And so the dumbbells played dumb while the junior geniuses, basking in official glory, coasted lazily along.

The Teacher loved to teach. It was — clearly — the sugar syrup of his life. When he lectured, he was addressing not us alone but the whole world. A select member of the human condition, he loomed over us in the solitude of that responsibility, and without really seeing us, or even taking us into account, he beat the barbarians of this earth over the head with the gospel of universal values. Sometimes he entered the classroom weighed down by domestic misfortune, racked by a hollow cough, and then perked up as the lesson progressed, as though revived by the chalk, the blackboard, his books open on the desk, the knowledge pouring from his lips. Sustained by a wrenching energy, he seemed to contend fiercely before our eyes with the Shadow that hung heavily over humanity. Sweeping gestures. Ringing pronouncements. Smacks on the desks with his ruler. This energy also fueled rambling digressions on Peace, dictatorships, Nazi concentration camps, the conscience of science, the Bomb, assembly-line work, Social Security, American power . . . Sometimes, acknowledging that he was a black man after all, he would rail at South Africa, the Ku Klux Klan, the martyrdom of Patrice Lumumba — then retreat into limpid humanism, that lofty height from which he delivered his verdicts. When the bell rang, he would dismiss us with a tired wave. Our savage dash for freedom and the playground seemed to depress him even more: he watched our jostling herd with the vague feeling of having wasted his time. But it didn't last. Out in the courtyard with the other Teachers, anxious to appear strong, he would take his place on parade while trying, like his colleagues, to take up as much space as possible.

"We do not say, to give *out of spite*. We say, to give *generously . . .*"

The Teacher was still the Teacher out in the street. He did not walk like everyone else. His bearing was more sober, as though he were obliged at every instant to confront life's realities with merciless lucidity. People looked at him. Greeted him. Crossed the street to touch his hand. Tried to engage him in the smallest of small talk, but he listened with only half an ear and never checked his severely measured tread. Unlike the common run of mankind, he had no fear of automobiles. He would step into the street without really looking, simply raising one admonitory finger, and his aura was so powerful that the worst road hogs would screech to a halt in silent fury, glaring while he crossed to the other sidewalk with never a glance in their direction.

"What do you mean, dear frriend, when you write, *He sugared up his coffee*? Does that mean he sweetened it?"

Each pupil was dosed with medicine by his mama to help him face the Teacher. Depending on the effect of these secret potions, this or that boy might stride into the classroom with a hint of extra vim. We were still children, however, and the best of intentions could come to grief. Our bodies played tricks on us. We'd learned to keep them seated on a bench, but they escaped us in many ways. One boy would find himself surprised by a flood of peepee right in the middle of class. His hand, raised to seek permission for the toilet, had merely accompanied the deluge. Another boy, who'd been lethargic all morning long, would suddenly sit up straight, enveloped in the most hateful perfume. His bench mate would start bellowing bloody murder, and a joyous panic would surge through his nearest neighbors, who'd all look as though they'd been punched in the nose. The shit-pants would sit glued to his seat by the pestiferous porridge oozing out beneath him. The Teacher—magnanimously—would enlist one of his favorites to take the little stinker to the infirmary. After seeing the culprit off with a gloomy eye, the Teacher would return pensively to the blackboard. He cast that same bleak look at those whose noses continually extruded a thin green stream, or those unfortunates whose legs were peppered with the tiny wheals we called hot spots and who spent their time slumped against their desks, scratching, scratching, scratching . . . To the Teacher, these symptoms must have seemed the somatization of his enemy, ignorance. Our piddles, diarrheas, and hives served him as markers to evaluate the scope of his task. And to judge from his fatigue, he was nowhere near beginning to see his way clear.

O *Répondeurs*, get me out of there . . .

Big Bellybutton had given up. He no longer tried to ask a question or even to answer one of the Teacher's posers. He didn't join in the arithmetic sessions, either. His lovely gift for numbers had disintegrated in the boredom that now overwhelmed him. His body had lost its sap: no more finger-fiddling, leg-swinging, or heel-tapping. Exhausted, he let the hours in class slip by while he dozed under cover, behind wide-open eyes: needless camouflage, since the Teacher never even noticed his torpor anymore. The Teacher now moved from pet to pet, halfheartedly soliciting participation from the rest of the class, returning immediately to his favorites in the front rows. Sometimes, inflamed by righteous wrath, he would pounce on some lost cause in the back of the class, savaging him six ways from Sunday, predicting a sinister future for him in the sugarcane fields, in the clutches of the *békés* . . . And then he would abandon the lost cause once again—until the next time his conscience prickled him.

Big Bellybutton had called it quits. He seemed to have accepted what the Teacher had decided he was. He had lost that wild resilience the little boy had admired in him at difficult moments—the lively eye, the firmly set chin, the compactness of his body braced for class. Watching him out of the corner of his eye, the little boy witnessed (he must have been the only one) the impalpable destruction of Big Bellybutton. The child was absent: absent from class, absent from himself. No longer to be seen frolicking exuberantly through recess or doing battle on the triangles. He never lingered anymore to have a choice word with us, distill a proverb, give us shivers with a tale. His body drifted around the water faucets or the entrance gate like a zombie-yawl. The candy lady would hand him a soursweet tamarind ball—most unusual behavior—and harangue him in old-timey Creole with a worried look on her face. She seemed to be trying to bar his way out. But from then on, Big Bellybutton kept his face turned toward the winds, toward life, longing to wipe out the failure of this childhood, these school days—oh, to grow up quickly, quickly, and move on to a different beat . . .

Répondeurs:
He was picking up his marbles!

Big Bellybutton had picked up his marbles and gone home. The Teacher never noticed a thing. He would have had to look, or to have known how to look, or to have had the time to look. He saw only grim little Big Bellybutton, balkier than ever, impervious to punishments, blows, suspensions, increasingly don't-givva-damn about the lessons. But the little boy, now, sitting right next to him—he saw, he saw, oh nothing, just a shudder, just the confusion and distress in Big Bellybutton's eye when he glanced at his neighbor. Fleeting collapses. Unspoken farewells. Glimpsed yet unseen.

Répondeurs:
Even without growing up
—a different beat!

As for the little boy, he'd fallen into the same lethargy. School was leaching all the curiosity from his mind. He came alive only on the way home, or in the sumptuous excitement of the triangles, or on the playground, trading treasures with other youngsters during recess. When he reached home, however, he found an atmosphere of studious yet enticing activity. The Baroness, Marielle, Paul the Musician, and Jojo the Math Whiz would be settled at the dining-room table. Mam Ninotte would be standing by the small spirit stove frying up some jackfish or browning vegetables for a meatless soup. Everyone spread their pen and pencil cases, notebooks, papers, and books out on the table. They all did their homework, checked it over, and asked for help when they hit snags. The Baroness did her own assignments and supervised those of the others. Rather: their work was hers as well. She took care of her sister and brothers without any prompting from Mam Ninotte, as if they were her own children or another part of herself, with a devotion that will remain steadfast her whole life long. She possessed a clarity of judgment that would come to us only with time, and her war against poverty was fought on all fronts. Baroness shortchanged of childhood, O precocious woman warrior . . .

The Baroness knew how to root out listlessness, shake up a lazybones, and run things with a firm hand. She neglected nothing, lost nothing, threw nothing away. She understood the worth of a heel of stale bread, a last dollop of cream, an old exercise book. From a shred of cloth, she could whip herself up a dress; the least little rag became an elegant outfit. And she knew how to put a good face on life with artful touches: an egg, a bit of flour, a lick of sugar — *cookies!* She plowed a straight furrow, unaffected by caprice, and more than one scatterbrain thought her hardhearted.

Répondeurs:
O Baroness of my heart . . .

(Baroness, at the cost of your childhood, you kept ours safe . . .)

The little boy was excluded from this studious gathering. So he decided to join it. There he is, scribbling on his slate. That's him, badgering the Baroness for some paper to write on. It's really him, frowning with pretended concentration, mimicking the others the better to fit in. When he acquired his own little school assignments, he was at last able to slip proudly under the authority of the Baroness and share the experience of homework with his brothers and sisters . . . until the Papa would get hungry and pronounce it time to eat.

At that table, the little boy saw his brothers' and sisters' school-books and began to covet them. The Teacher had already impressed him by the care he took of books; the little boy was astonished to see them treated so casually by Paul or Jojo the Math Whiz. They bent the pages, doodled in them, picked them up by one flap. Marielle dried flower petals in them. Only the Baroness, meticulous in everything, showed any special consideration for them, but nothing like the Teacher's devotion. Through the years, the Big Kids had received other books as progress or achievement awards, works by Jules Verne, Daniel Defoe, Alexandre Dumas, Lewis Carroll, the Comtesse de Ségur, R. L. Stevenson . . . Mam Ninotte kept them in a box she allowed her youngest to dip into; only the textbooks were off-limits. He would pretend to read the others, leafing through the pages, dazzled by the illustrations — truly, it was a touching sight. Without encouraging him, his family left him to it.

Book in hand, imitating the Teacher's slow, respectful gestures: opening it delicately, holding it lovingly, putting on that affected look over the first sentence, flipping through the pages as though searching for something vital, stopping to reflect on who-knows-what . . . The little boy was a master of macaquery. That's him, spending more and more time enthralled by the magic crate that brought him unknowingly closer to the Teacher. There he is, badgering the Baroness to explain some picture to him: *What is this? What's happening here? Why's that there?* . . . And the Baroness would explain. And re-explain. But the explanations (usually partial) were more tantalizing still. He'd survey the tiny, indecipherable letters, straining to recognize one or the other of them, recognizing a word, a syllable, going all the way to the last page — then he'd come back, pull out another book . . .

A book, to him, was a phantasmagorical object. Mam Ninotte, now — she saw them as tabernacles of knowledge. She never forbade him to touch them, handle them, line them up, stack them, pretend to read them. When she discovered his interest, she began bringing home from the fish market (a *djobeur* there used to sell off all kinds of papers piled in a big wheelbarrow) anything that vaguely resembled a book: newspapers, almanacs, comics, detective stories, photonovels, everything . . . The little boy welcomed all printed material with the same greedy delight.

The bookcase was a potato crate made of white wooden slats bound together with wire. Mam Ninotte had stuffed it into the bottom of a wardrobe, beneath some shrouds. Time-to-time, the little boy would startle a mouse that had nibbled the sweet glue on a binding. He would sound the alarm, shrieking blue murder, chasing the beastly thing under the cupboard, and tracking it beneath the beds. His distress didn't arouse any particular reinforcements. Mam Ninotte would simply curse she-rats and all their progeny, while the Baroness never said a word. Everyone seemed to think that once read, a book was finished. They were kept the way tin cans, bottles, papers were saved: for a *just-in-case* . . . It was hard to pin down Mam Ninotte's interest in them, as they hardly came in handy during the runaround of daily life. She just kept them, that's all, in the name of Education.

The books in the crate were preserved under a layer of dust. Their paper had turned yellow and a bit brittle. They were as crackly as bamboo in a drought. Less than assiduous reading had not worn them out, but passing cockroaches had left their mark. The books seemed to have come almost intact from a different age. Sometimes the little boy had the impression they had emerged from the fabulous worlds depicted in their own illustrations. When you picked one up, it clung to the others with spider webs. And when you opened them — when you opened them, the ruffled paper breathed a sort of ancient sigh, *oh, when you opened them* . . .

To reach the crate, you had to plunge into the desolate darkness, beneath the clothing in the wardrobe, with a pounding heart. You were dragging a treasure chest from a grotto . . .

The little boy rewrote the books according to the pictures, inventing stories that he then tried to find in the printed (and still indecipherable) text. Soon he didn't need diddly in the way of help from anyone: he made up his own narratives, spread them out among the incomprehensible letters, and followed them vaguely from sentence to sentence like that until the end. He learned to develop an event to make it correspond to the number of lines on a page. He discovered how to launch himself from one picture and carry on until he reached the next one. He seemed to be pretending to read, when in fact he really was reading what his frenzied imagination projected each time upon the page. His initial dabble in make-believe (intended to make him seem more grownup) became a pleasant necessity that nurtured his adventurous mind.

The books still kept secrets his imagination could not make up for, however. When he had finished his story, the text would recover its cryptic placidity. The book became compact once again. Shut up tight. That's why he was particularly attentive during the Teacher's vocabulary sessions and began to grasp the words, use them, remember them, add them to his everyday conversation. He noticed that new French words produced quite an effect: Mam Ninotte opened her eyes wide in proud amazement, while the Baroness squinted hers down to slits, checking to be sure he knew what the word meant. Even Jojo the Math Whiz, off in his numerical nirvana, rolled an eye at him. Bit by bit by bit, the homey little Creole in his head was joined by scraps of French, words, phrases . . . There was no looking back . . .

*Répondeurs, je ne suis pas bien là . . .**

*A ritual phrase with which a storyteller signals that his tale is almost done, that another *conteur* should now speak up. (Translator's note.)

The mystery of books made him pay close attention to the classroom writing lessons—to understand how all this worked. His handwriting wasn't very good; his upstrokes and downstrokes were never perfect. The Teacher spied every ink stain on his fingers and his work and punished him for the disaster area around his inkwell. The Teacher yelped, threatened, crammed the margins of his pages with exclamation points, but the little boy remained unfazed. He was fascinated by this a b c x y z business, this great array of letters and the potential he already sensed in them for endless combinations. He tackled them with delight, not to please the Teacher but for his own pleasure. Bowed over his pages of writing, he experienced real moments of happiness: the pen scratching along, opening a curve, giving birth to a letter that hesitates ... and closes up, imprisoning its meaning—now redo it, watch it come out different, and try again, botch it up, get it almost right ... Big Bellybutton would watch him apathetically from the corner of his eye.

What did he see, this master of Creole?

What did he see, this child who would soon leave his school days far behind?

Not much, probably.

He would have needed the ancient gift of second sight to divine that—in this sacking of their native world, in this crippling inner ruination—the little black boy bent over his notebook was tracing, without fully realizing it, an inky lifeline of survival ...

Répondeurs:
Storytellers, on your mark!
Ho: off you go!

Favorite, 21 January 1994

Glossary

awa: An exclamation of disbelief, disappointment.

Balata: The Jardin de Balata, named for a hardwood tree related to the sapodilla, is a botanical park just north of Fort-de-France.

bawoufer: "To snatch with a grasping hand" (*Texaco*).

béké ("beaky," "honky"): A white person whose family has lived in Martinique for generations. The *békés* formed a powerful, endogamous elite, and until very recently they kept their social distance from nonwhites. A *gwo-béké* (a big *béké*) is rich while a *béké-goyave* (a guava *béké*) is not, but the *békés'* sense of community ensured that no white Martinican fell into real poverty.

Bête-à-Man-Ibè: Mother Hubert's Monster, a bogy in Martinican folk tales.

caco: Chocolate colored.

chabin: Someone with light coloring, "high yellow."

chaleur (heat): Uh-oh! Things are heating up! Trouble!

chenille-trèfle: A caterpillar found on clover; its black oil is considered a universal counterpoison.

chi-chine, kouli: After Emancipation in the French Antilles, the freed slaves took to the land, and people from many different parts of the world were brought in to work on the sugar plantations. The immigrants from India, or *koulis*, who constituted by far the largest group of indentured laborers, further complicated the pattern of social and race relations in the Caribbean. Two other groups of new arrivals were the Chinese (*chi-chine, chin-wa*), who tended to enter small shopkeeping, and the Syrians and Lebanese, who specialized in retailing cloth, clothes, and household goods.

Downtown (*l'En-ville*): Implies the idea of a project rather than a simple destination, as in the Barbadian expression "goin' down in Town."

fer: Damn! That's hard! That's tough!

Gros Kato: The North Star.

isalop: Idiot, little bastard.

la chaux (quicklime): As Chamoiseau explains in *Texaco*, this is an announcement that life is about to burn someone.

Makandal: A legendary Haitian leader who waged a campaign of terror against the French planters of the colony of Saint Domingue in the late eighteenth century. The endless stories of how Makandal would miraculously escape from his enemies by transforming himself into a bird, a fire, or a wolf are central to the Caribbean oral tradition.

Mam: The Creole for *Madame* is actually *Man*—which, for obvious reasons, became *Mam* in this English translation, with the author's approval.

morne (French West Indies): A small, round hill.

quimboiseur, quimboiseuse: Seer, fetish priest or priestess who practices a form of witchcraft related to obeah and voodoo.

Répondeurs: Chamoiseau's cheeky "back-talkers"—part Muses, part Greek chorus in a call-and-response mode.

roye/woy: Ouch! Watch out! Oy-oy-oy!

Schoelcher, Victor: A Parisian-born deputy from Alsace who was instrumental in freeing Martinique's slaves in 1848.

soucougnan: An old woman who turns into a ball of fire at night and sucks the blood of humans; a sorcerer who sheds his skin to work evil on his victims (the word supposedly means "master of the moonless night" in Dahoman).

stoppin'-coffin (*cercueil-arrêteur*): A coffin that bars the way.

three-leg-horse (*chouval-twa-pattes*): A ghost horse that pulled a hearse in life.

ziggedy (*ziguidi*): A *baakoo*, a spirit in a bottle, who can be fiercely disruptive if he escapes from his prison.

UNIVERSITY OF GLAMORGAN
PRIFYSGOL MORGANNWG
Learning Resources Centre

For further information about Granta Books
and a full list of titles, please write to us at

Granta Books

2/3 HANOVER YARD

NOEL ROAD

LONDON

N1 8BE

enclosing a stamped, addressed envelope

———————————

You can visit our website at

http://www.granta.com